When Winter Is Past

Janice Cole Hopkins

Published by Flawed People Press
Gilbert, Arizona

Produced in the United States of America

Edited by C. S. Lakin

Other Books by Janice Cole Hopkins

Appalachian Root Series

Cleared for Planting (Book 1)
Sown in Dark Soil (Book 2)
Uprooted by War (Book 3)

"For, lo, the winter is past, the rain is over and gone."

—Song of Solomon 2:11

Chapter One: The Search Begins

"A house without woman and firelight is like a body without soul or spirit."

— Poor Richard's Almanack

Pennsylvania, May 1739

Stanton Klein sat on the ground beside the grave and leaned his back against a tree. The dampness from the recent rain seeped into him, but he paid it little mind. His eyes were fixed on the grave; yet they saw the past year through the dense fog that surrounded the farm.

It had been a hard year since his Molly had died in childbirth. He had wanted a child more than anything. He needed a son to help him on the farm, carry on his name, and inherit his holdings. The infant girl had died with his wife. It hadn't even been a boy, for all the trouble it'd brought. He'd buried them both in the same grave.

He had waited almost a year, the longest year of his life, but he wanted to show his respect for his deceased wife. Time had frozen that winter, and he hoped he never had to live through another like it. As soon as Molly had been buried and the visitors left, things got as difficult as steerage passage across the Atlantic. After all the initial upheaval, everyone else's lives went back to normal, but his remained upturned, and, in the quiet, it hit him full force.

He brushed his eyes and blinked. Even at the start of the day, he felt tired. Sleep didn't visit for long anymore. It remained elusive, something he hunted but could no longer track down. Regardless of how long and hard he worked, he stayed awake at night more often than not.

At twenty-eight years of age, he needed to marry again. A man needed a wife—and a farmer needed one more than most. He needed a son. If he started looking now, maybe he would be able to marry before the busy harvest time arrived. He'd have two or three months until the fields demanded his full attention. If things were delayed, he'd just have to wait until after the harvest, but he was determined to be married before the cold weather set in again. He refused to spend another dismal winter shivering alone.

He'd met Molly in Philadelphia. She'd never fit into farm life as much as he would have liked. She hated all the outdoor chores, but she'd kept a clean house, cooked their meals, sewed their clothes, and did the laundry and other household tasks. They'd gotten along well enough.

He knew he'd never loved her, but he'd cared for her and grieved at her passing. He had vowed long ago to never love a woman. His father had given his heart away to Stanton's mother, and when she died in childbirth, his father had withered away and followed her to the grave by his own hand. Stanton never forgave his father for deserting him like that. Why hadn't his son been enough to live for? No, Stanton never wanted to love like that. He had been ten at the time, and he'd had his grandparents, but that wasn't the same as having parents. His father had been a surprise for Stanton's grandparents and was much younger than his siblings. He and his parents had emigrated from Germany, leaving the older brother with the farm there. The older brother and three sisters were already married with families of their own in the Old Country.

Stanton's grandparents had established a farm to the west of Philadelphia. At first, it had been tough trying to create a home in the wilderness, but with hard work and perseverance, they'd managed to create a good life. His father had met and married a local girl, and by the time Stanton took over, the farm had been doing well. He could offer his wife a good life.

He rubbed his itching eyes, and the grave came into clear view again, bringing him back to the present. He hoped he could find a wife in the village. All the unmarried neighbors' daughters he knew were too young for marriage, but he didn't want to have to go to Philadelphia again.

Being twenty-eight years old, he didn't want a wife too much younger than himself. Sure, some older men married young teens, but he couldn't see himself with anyone more than ten years younger. He didn't want some silly giggling girl who had nothing in common with him. He preferred a serene, responsible young lady, except most of them were already married. Perhaps God would aid him in his search. God had taken Molly from him, so, the way Stanton saw it, He should be obligated to help him find another.

He shrugged off the thought. He tried to think of God as little as possible now. Where had He been when Stanton had struggled through the cold, lonely days and nights? Where was the comfort promised in the Bible? Why had Molly been taken so young, for that matter? If God wanted to leave him alone, then Stanton would leave God alone too.

"Don't put a question mark where God puts a period," he could hear his grandfather say.

His grandmother would tell him: if we don't understand why something happens, then we should just trust God more. He missed his family. In the back of his mind, he felt they'd be disappointed in how he'd pulled back from God. Surely he had time to work this all out. Perhaps a godly wife would help.

He shook his head and saw the fog had lifted. The sun had taken over, and the morning colors of fuchsia and purple made the sky appear bruised—like him. He must have been here longer than he'd realized. His thoughts had been flying around like wrens trying to run a small predator from their nest. If he planned to go into Middleville today, he'd better get moving.

"You need any help in town today?" Ralph McCarthy asked him.

He looked at his indentured servant. Oftentimes he didn't feel comfortable leaving the young man at the farm by himself, but he had nothing firm to base that on, and he shook off the feeling.

"No, you best stay here today. The fields are always in need of weeding, and I won't be hauling that much back."

Ralph nodded, almost losing the hat from his fiery-red head in the process. The sun seemed to make his freckles multiply by the minute.

Stanton had bought Ralph's indenture after Frank Coddle had served out his bondage and left. Frank had been indentured while his grandfather still lived, and the old man had no longer been able to work. Stanton had liked Frank. In fact, he'd paid Frank wages to stay on for a while, but the man had saved some money and set out to make his own way. He'd married well, had a farm of his own in another county, and had sons to help him.

The trip to Middleville didn't take long because the town had grown up a few miles from the Klein farm. Stanton liked the convenience. Although not a large town, when compared to Philadelphia, Stanton only knew some of its inhabitants, mainly the ones who went to the Lutheran church with him. He didn't go to town to socialize like some did, and the farm kept him busy.

He breathed in and filled his lungs. The air always smelled fresher after a rain. By noon, though, it would be warm enough, yet the day had turned out to be a beautiful one.

Where to begin? He'd start with his minister. Reverend Durk knew most of the people in the village, even if they didn't attend his church.

Although Stanton might not have been on the best terms with God, he'd continued to attend church—when the weather permitted. It provided a chance for him to get out of the house, which had begun to feel more like a cold, dark tomb. He could have gone to the tavern sometime, but Stanton knew, considering the way he'd felt, if he'd begun to drink, brew might become a habit he couldn't break with ease. On cold, blustery days most men enjoyed a warm mug of flip, and many couldn't stop at one.

"Come in, come in." The minister seemed pleased to see him. "It's not often we see you here in the middle of the week. What brings you to town?"

Stanton entered the roomy clapboard and greeted the minister. Reverend Durk had to be nearing middle age. He had recently gained a little weight around his midsection, and his brown hair had grayed at his temples.

"I wanted to speak to you. I'm thinking of taking a wife."

"Well it's about time. Bertha and I agree it's past time you did so. I respect that you've waited almost a year, but things are different here than in the Old Country, and a farmer needs a wife. I think any man does, for that matter. Why, Abraham Schmidt took a new wife two months after his first wife died, and no one said anything about it. Of course, he had a multitude of young ones to worry about."

"Do you have any suggestions about where I might start?"

Reverend Durk's eyes twinkled with amusement. "There's always the Widow Knotts. She's seemed interested in you ever since Molly died."

Stanton winced. "She's interested in any available man who can support her."

The pastor raised his eyebrows, and Stanton realized how critical his remark sounded. "I mean, she's too forward for my tastes." He wondered if he'd only made matters worse by trying to rectify his comment.

"I see. There's always Fiona Fletcher, but you need to move fast if you decide to court her. She's attractive and quite sought after. Her family attends the Presbyterian church if you want to seek her out. How young are you willing to consider?"

"I don't think I've ever met Miss Fletcher, and, to be honest, I wouldn't want a wife much less than eighteen and certainly no one younger than sixteen."

"Fiona is seventeen. I don't know of anyone else who's older than fifteen and not married already. Oh, there's Beth Evans, who's nineteen, but she's deformed with one leg shorter than the other, and she's the only one who can take care of her invalid father. I hear he's not doing well, though. I don't visit them, since they aren't members of our congregation. You might want to talk to Agatha Denny. She knows everyone around, and she might know of someone I've missed."

Agatha Denny was the town's gossipmonger. If he talked with her, everyone would know he was looking for a wife. That might be okay as a last resort, but he'd forego that situation for now. It sounded as if he'd start with Fiona Fletcher. He liked that name,

Chapter Two: Fiona

"Meanness is the parent of insolence."

—Poor Richard's Almanack

Stanton went to the merchant's shop. He always purchased a few goods when he came to Middleville, and perhaps he could catch a glimpse of Miss Fletcher here.

As he walked through the door, he saw Mr. Mueller talking with Cecil Shippen. Stanton didn't know the young man well, but what he did know, he didn't like. Cecil tried to be the ladies' man and had an inflated idea of himself.

"I hear you've about made another conquest?" Mr. Mueller said.

"To which are you referring?" young Shippen asked. Without doubt, he insinuated there could be more than one.

Stanton went to a candle display, where he wouldn't be in the direct vision of the two men. He would need some candles soon, since he had no one to make them now.

"I hear Miss Fletcher is quite taken with you."

Stanton's head jerked up. Was the lady's interest already engaged? Would Fiona think Stanton too old for her, and would he come up short when compared to Cecil Shippen?

"What can I say? With a little attention, I can have any unmarried lady in the county and a few married ones as well. I guess it's a talent I have."

Stanton frowned in disgust. He felt like leaving the premises, but he also felt compelled to hear what they had to say about Miss Fletcher.

"Are there wedding plans in the making, then?" Mr. Mueller sounded as if he already knew the answer.

"No, I'm not ready to settle down yet, but I do love the courting."

"You'd better watch it, or you'll ruin your reputation and theirs. Ladies from a good family, like Fiona Fletcher, are not to be toyed with. Her father has influence around here. Until you're serious, you need to stick with the tavern wenches."

"Oh, I have no intention of getting trapped. If I like a woman enough, I'll just have her wait for me, till I'm ready for a wife and family. I'm but twenty-two now, so I have a few years left before I need to become yoked."

Stanton looked at Cecil. He supposed the young man would be considered handsome. He stood about five foot nine and likely had light-blond hair beneath the wig he wore. At least his pallid eyebrows gave that indication. His pale-blue eyes sparkled with mischief, and he appeared fit. His family seemed to have money, if his clothing gave any indication, and Stanton would bet they'd spoiled their son.

After what he'd heard, did he need to reassess his interest in Fiona? Maybe Cecil had exaggerated his involvement with her. He seemed the sort to stretch things in his favor.

Stanton bought the few items he needed and headed home. As he rode out of town, he noticed a pretty young woman walking in the village with an older woman, probably her mother. Could that be Fiona? He didn't get a good look, but he liked what he saw. She was dressed in light-blue trimmed in white, and with her coloring, he guessed her eyes would also be blue. Her hair glowed a golden blond, and she carried herself erect and in a graceful manner, which almost made her seem to float.

Stanton rode on by. After what he'd heard at the store today, he wanted to give the matter some more thought, and it would be better if he could get someone to introduce him to her family. Otherwise, he might appear too forward or even uncouth.

He needed to visit the Presbyterian church on Sunday, for that's where most of the non-German folk went to church. He felt sure he could spot Fiona and her family there.

Stanton knew Middleville boasted of only three main religious groups: the Lutherans, the Presbyterians, and the Society of Friends or Quakers. No Anglican church had been built in their village. There were two small churches—the Lutheran and the Presbyterian. The Quakers met in homes and didn't have a church building. He hoped Reverend Durk had been right and Fiona attended the Presbyterian.

On Sunday, Stanton dressed in his best suit of clothes. He asked Ralph if he wanted to go to the Presbyterian church with him, but the servant declined. He and Ralph got along well enough, but they weren't close, as he and Frank had been. He hadn't told Ralph about his quest for a wife.

He considered taking the wagon and asking Fiona to go for a ride with him, but he decided against it. He would just assess the situation today and ask to call if things looked promising.

After he arrived at the white, clapboard building, he stood outside to talk with some of the men. Cecil stood at the edge of the churchyard with a group of younger men. Stanton frowned. He might have known Shippen would show up, but then he scolded himself. The cad needed to be in church from what he'd seen.

He heard someone call "Fiona" and looked up. She, her parents, and a younger brother got out of a carriage. She had been the woman he'd seen walking in Middleville earlier, and she looked even prettier than he'd thought. She had those vibrant blue eyes beneath honey-blond hair, and a heart-shaped face, but she looked older than seventeen. There seemed to be an air of sophistication about her. She looked poised and self-assured. Stanton's heart quickened at the thought of this beautiful woman possibly becoming his.

Today she wore a dress of lavender silk that must have been shipped from the Continent. It flattered her flawless cream-colored skin and made her look almost regal. She glanced at him, paused, and gave him a coy smile. Did it show her interest in him? Was she flirting? His heart started racing, and his knees suddenly grew weaker than they should have been.

Stanton saw Cecil give Fiona a wicked smile, but she didn't acknowledge him, as she walked into the church with her family. Perhaps the interest rested with Cecil and not Fiona. His pulse quickened.

Stanton noted the service seemed less formal than his, and he liked the preacher's enthusiasm, but he had to admit, he heard little of the message. His mind had been on one young lady and how to meet her. It would be best if he could find somcone to introduce him.

When the service ended, Stanton watched Fiona go outside with some of the girls, while her parents lingered inside. Stanton headed for the door, where the minister stood talking with people as they left, but Stanton lingered for a moment. He timed it so he would leave near the Fletchers.

"So glad to have you with us, Mr. Klein. I was sorry to hear of your loss." The minister shook his hand. Reverend Carr looked older than Reverend Durk, but he appeared spry and in good health.

Stanton tried to hide his surprise. He didn't know the Presbyterian minister even knew his name, much less his situation.

"Thank you. It's been a long ten months, and I need to be getting out and meeting more people."

"Of course you do. I hope you'll join us again."

"It would be my pleasure."

"Do you know Mr. and Mistress Fletcher?"

Stanton turned around to see the older couple behind him. They both wore wigs and looked rotund. "I don't believe I've had the pleasure."

"Stanton Klein, may I present Donald and Mary Fletcher."

The Fletchers seemed surprised at the pastor's brief introduction. "Nice to meet you," they said as Mr. Fletcher put out his hand.

"The pleasure is all mine," Stanton told them.

"Mr. Klein is a widower and has a nice farm a few miles out," the minister added.

The Fletchers looked at him with renewed interest. He knew they were taking in the cut and fabric of his suit. He hadn't worn a wig, for he hated the feel of the things, but otherwise he felt he'd pass their inspection.

"Would you like to meet our daughter?" Mistress Fletcher asked. "We need to gather the children and be off for home."

Stanton hesitated a moment. Was he ready for this? "I would be delighted." He needed to make some decision about whether or not to court Fiona, and this visit would help.

As they approached the group of four girls, one pulled away with a look of dismay. She turned and walked away with as much speed as she could muster with her limp.

"She'll never find a man who'll marry her with that deformed leg," Fiona snapped loud enough for the young woman to hear. "She's cursed to become a spinster."

Stanton looked at Fiona, amazed at her audacity and rudeness. He'd hoped her character would match her lovely physical attributes. Then, he turned to observe the other young woman.

She kept walking and didn't turn. Stanton sifted through his memory to remember the name of the young woman with the limp Reverend Durk had mentioned.

Cecil had been standing nearby watching Fiona. He took a short step back when he heard Fiona's cutting words. "Your tongue is much too sharp today, Miss Fletcher," he said. "Why are you spewing your venom at the less fortunate?"

"What is it to you, Mr. Shippen? Are you interested in Miss Evans?"

Evans. Beth Evans. That was her name.

"Ah, my dear. You know you're the one for me," Cecil answered.

Mr. Fletcher cleared his throat, and Fiona blushed. Cecil tipped his hat and walked away.

Stanton wondered why the world tended to herd everyone to the middle. People were critical of those who didn't conform to the general population. They didn't like anyone who tended to be different, like too fat, too short, too dumb, too poor, and the list could go on and on. They didn't like Beth Evans because she limped. Stanton didn't understand it. He'd seen the look of hurt on Beth's face as she limped away, and his heart went out to her.

When Mr. Fletcher introduced Stanton to Fiona, she stared at him with even more intensity than her mother had. She looked him over, like a queen born to rule over everyone and with every right to do so. Then she curtsied and whispered, "Enchanted, Mr. Klein."

He bowed. "As I am, Miss Fletcher."

Her eyes fluttered, and Stanton wondered at the young woman's adeptness at flirtation. She moistened her lips with her tongue, and he knew then she had perfected the art.

The more he saw of her, the more he wondered whether he should consider pursuing her or not. Her looks were the only thing he'd found interesting so far, and those would not be important in the shadow of a harsh, haughty personality.

"Would you care to dine with us, Mr. Klein?" Mr. Fletcher asked. "I feel we should become better acquainted."

Stanton considered Mr. Fletcher's invitation. After what he'd seen this morning, he wondered if he should decline. However, he needed to make sure. Perhaps Fiona had just overreacted to some negative comment Beth Evans had made.

"I would love to if you're sure it won't be too much trouble."

"No trouble at all," Mistress Fletcher told him. "We like to have company, and I always have plenty prepared. I hope a simple stew will suffice. It's easier for Sunday after church."

"Anything sounds better than my meager attempt at a meal," he told her.

"Good, it's settled then. Just follow our carriage. It isn't far."

On the way to the Fletchers, Stanton couldn't rein in his conflicting thoughts. On one hand, he felt an attraction to Fiona that he couldn't deny. He'd love to have such a pretty woman as his wife. On the other hand, he wanted nothing to do with a shrew, and he would need to take care. Once he asked to court her, everyone would assume they would marry, and it would be much harder to extract himself from a bad situation.

The Fletchers' house sat on a small rise just outside town. It looked a little larger than Stanton's, but this one had been constructed of clapboard and not stone. It had a chimney at either end, which meant more than one fireplace. By the look of the house, their carriage, and their clothes, the family had money. Would they welcome a farmer as a suitor for their daughter? Did he want to be one now that he'd seen Fiona's haughty side?

The meal progressed well. The conversation seemed a little uncomfortable to begin with, but Stanton answered their questions and asked some of his own. The food tasted as good as Molly might have prepared, and it felt good to sit down and eat a hot meal. He tended to survive on cold meats and bread now that he fixed his own meals.

At first, the families from church had invited him to eat with them as often as he came to town. The invitations had slowed now, however, although the Widow Knotts had kept them coming. He declined those because he didn't want to encourage the woman. He suspected she entertained other men as well, but she'd made it clear she would welcome his attention.

Agnes Knotts, an attractive woman in her early thirties, had strawberry-blond hair and gray eyes, and she used her well-curved figure as an advantage to attract men. She owned a small cottage in the village, which she'd inherited from her first husband, but people speculated on how she maintained funds to manage her household. Stanton tried to avoid her as much as possible.

Fiona said little during the meal, but she listened and watched. She looked even more attractive without her bonnet. Stanton could find no flaw in her physical appearance, but he worried about her nature. He wouldn't care to find himself with an ill-tempered wife.

"Fiona, would you like to show Mr. Klein the garden? I think most of the spring flowers are still in bloom," Mistress Fletcher asked after the meal.

"I find myself developing a terrible headache and need to lie down now," Fiona replied. She turned to Stanton. "Perhaps another time, Mr. Klein."

"Of course."

Stanton didn't know what to think. He had thought Fiona had shown interest in him. Now, he wasn't so sure.

Fiona excused herself and climbed the stairs. Mr. Fletcher invited Stanton into the parlor, while Mistress Fletcher cleaned the kitchen.

"We have a maid, but she has Sundays off," Mistress Fletcher told him as he rose.

He didn't ask if the help was indentured or hired. It didn't matter to him. Perhaps he should get an indentured female to help his new wife. He should at least consider it.

It felt cooler in the parlor than the kitchen, and the two men talked in more comfort. Stanton liked Donald Fletcher just fine, but he found it more difficult to make up his mind about the daughter. He wished they had walked in the garden. That would have given him a better idea about Fiona's real nature and if he'd be interested in pursuing a courtship with her.

Stanton left as soon as he thought he could do so without appearing rude. As he rode away, he saw Fiona slip out the back and head for a wooded area behind her house. He also thought he saw a male figure tucked into the shadows of the trees. Was the chit meeting a man, perhaps Cecil Shippen? He hoped she wouldn't sneak out alone and ruin her reputation or worse. He certainly wasn't ready to begin courting her now, but should he give up the idea entirely? As Reverend Durk had indicated, single women of a marriageable age were in short supply.

The following night presented more difficulties than usual. Stanton's loneliness pressed down with extra weight, and he lay deep in thought throughout the night. Fiona's beauty pulled at him, and he felt sure he would find no other to match her attractiveness. Yet, she'd been cruel and harsh with Beth Evans, and she appeared to be sneaking out for a clandestine meeting. He wanted no part of the trouble those things could cause. He felt torn. A part of him wanted to have such a beauty for his wife, but another part ordered caution and even retreat.

The rest of the week went no better. He and Ralph worked hard, but Stanton still got little sleep. By Sunday morning, he had no idea which church to attend. At least going to the Presbyterian one kept him away from the widow's advances.

Stanton entered the Presbyterian church with a sense of trepidation. His indecision had caused him to be later than he liked, and he slipped onto a bench near the back just as the service started. He could see the Fletchers near the front. Cecil sat just across the aisle from Fiona, and he kept looking her way. Fiona kept her gaze straight ahead.

He heard a rustle and looked up to see Beth Evans limp to the bench in front of him but on the opposite side of the church. He had a good view of her, since they both sat on the aisle end of their benches. She wore a dress of light-brown homespun linen, but it looked nice with her coloring and dark-brown hair. She appeared thin, but even from here he could see she had a comely figure. What was he doing? And in church of all places! He looked away, but he couldn't help wondering what color her eyes were.

The preacher delivered a message on watching the tongue. He told of the pain harsh words could cause and reminded the congregation that gossip was a sin. He went on to expound on the grave transgression of lying. Stanton wondered if Fiona had paid attention to the part about harsh words, but he still didn't know what his answer would be if the Fletchers asked him to dinner again.

He waited for Beth to leave first, and then walked out behind her. The minister took her hand and asked how her father fared.

"He didn't feel well this morning." Her voice came out soft and warm, like a summer breeze. "That's why I came in a bit late, but he insisted I come."

"I'll stop by and see him in the morning."

"Thank you, Reverend. He'll like that."

Reverend Carr put out his hand to Stanton. "It's good to see you again, Mr. Klein." Stanton saw Beth pause and turn back to see who the minister had addressed.

"Do you know Mr. Klein, Beth?" the reverend asked.

"No, I don't believe so." She stepped back toward them.

Green. Her eyes were a sparkling green.

"Stanton Klein, I'd like to present Beth Evans. She's a faithful soul to her father, her church, and her God."

"Then I am impressed indeed and pleased to meet you, Miss Evans."

"Thank you." She bobbed more than curtsied, then turned on stiff legs to walk away. Her limp seemed even more pronounced.

Stanton's eyes found Fiona immediately as he left the church, but she had her attention on Beth. He moved to the side to watch.

"Beth, come here," Fiona called. She sounded much more pleasant and friendly than she had before.

Beth hesitated, but then moved to the group of girls. Fiona greeted Beth with a big smile that never reached her eyes.

"Will you come to dinner at my house today?"

Beth had a questioning look on her face, as if she wondered what Fiona intended. Stanton wondered the same thing.

"Oh, come now," Fiona continued. "You know we're friends. I'm sorry for my foul mood last Sunday.

Cecil wants to come, but my parents will only permit it if they think Cecil is interested in someone else. Please help us out."

Beth shook her head. "I'd like to help, but I can't come."

"Please, Beth. When will you ever get another chance like this?"

"I'm not looking for a chance with Cecil, and I have to see to my father's dinner."

"Fine then! See when you ever have another chance to be in the company of an eligible young man!"

Beth turned without saying a word and limped away. Stanton had been standing back, but without thinking, he hurried forward to intercept Beth.

"Might I walk a short ways with you, Miss Evans? My horse is tied in this direction."

She looked as puzzled as she had when Fiona called her over. "I suppose so."

He presented his arm, and after a moment's hesitation, she slipped her hand into its crook. He slowed his pace to a slow stroll to match her stride.

"Why are you doing this, Mr. Klein?" She looked up at him, waiting for his response.

Stanton paused to wonder at her directness, but she sounded curious, not angry. He looked into her eyes and noticed the green had darkened a little. He wondered if they would darken yet again if she became angry.

"I couldn't help but hear what Miss Fletcher said to you, and I thought we'd show her you could have the chance to be in the company of an eligible man without her help."

Beth first looked surprised, and then she gave a genuine laugh. It washed over him, like a welcomed summer shower, and Stanton couldn't help but smile back.

"Are you eligible, Mr. Stanton?" The words could have been flirtatious, but she said them with interest, not flirtation.

"I've been a widower for almost a year now," he told her.

"I'm sorry." She sounded sincere, and her hand tightened on his arm.

"If you don't mind me asking, how do you manage the Miss Fletchers of this world and not let them send you away in tears? There are several things I'd like to say to her, but none of them are Christian."

"I remember Galatians 1:10. 'Seek to please God not men.' God gives me an undeserved sense of worth. I am His child first and foremost and a daughter of the King. There are those that will always try to tread on others in the hopes that it will elevate them."

"That's a very good way of looking at things," he said, as much to himself as her.

As they neared the post where he'd tied his horse, much to Stanton's regret, Beth pulled her hand away from his arm. Without doubt she planned to leave him, and he wanted her to stay.

"This must be your horse."

"It is, but I would be happy to walk you home."

"Thank you, but that won't be necessary. My house is nearby."

"Then it's been a pleasure to meet you, Miss Evans, and to be your escort, albeit for such a brief while."

She gave him a most radiant smile. "I've enjoyed your company, Mr. Klein, and thank you for helping to contradict Fiona's barb."

He mounted his horse and watched her limp away. He hoped she'd look back over her shoulder, but she didn't. He saw her go onto a stoop in a row of houses but couldn't tell its exact location. She turned her head toward him for a brief moment before she went inside, but she didn't wave, and he couldn't see the expression on her face from this distance. He turned his horse toward home.

Beth had been an unexpected pleasure, and he wished they could have talked longer. Should he consider courting her? He found her more interesting and more congenial than Fiona. And, although she wasn't as pretty, he thought her attractive enough. Her limp would only be a problem to Stanton if it could be inherited by any children.

Chapter Three: Beth

"Pray to God. Call no ill names. Love God. Use no ill words. Fear God. Tell no lies. Serve God. Hate Lies. Speak the Truth. Take not God's Name in vain. Spend your Time well."

—The New England Primer

"Mr. Klein! Mr. Klein!" Agatha Denny hurried toward him. Waddled would describe it better, for the woman must have weighed over two hundred pounds.

He dismounted his horse as a courtesy to her. Intuition told him it would be best to stay on her good side.

"Did I see you with Miss Evans?" She panted, trying to catch her breath.

"You did." The gossip mills would be turning now. "We came from church together but parted when I got to my horse."

"Yes, well, I see." He could see the disappointment in her face. The news wouldn't be worth telling. "I thought you went to the Lutheran church."

"I do. I just came here to visit. Do you know how Miss Evans got her limp? Was she born that way?"

"Oh, no. She broke her leg as a small child. That leg never grew to be the same length as the other, but before the accident, she ran about as she pleased. I believe she was about three when the accident occurred." Mistress Denny beamed as she imparted the information. One thing about Mistress Denny—she might overuse her tongue, but she took pride in being accurate. More often than not, one could trust what she said. What was it that his grandfather had always said? "Gossip isn't always right, but neither is it always wrong."

He rejoiced to hear Beth's deformity wasn't hereditary, so it wouldn't pass down to any children. He would certainly give Beth Evans some thought.

"Is Miss Evans the reason you're visiting the Presbyterian church?" Her eyes gleamed in eagerness for some new gossip she could spread around like fresh butter on oven-hot bread.

"No, madam. I came to observe Miss Fletcher. Her parents invited me to dinner last Sunday."

"Really?" Her eyes narrowed to slits. "You'd do better to pursue Miss Evans, despite her deformity. Beth Evans is a sweet soul, and no one who knows Miss Fletcher could say that about her. That one will bring trouble with her. You mark my words."

"I'll give your advice strong consideration, Mistress Denny." He didn't tell her he'd almost come to the same conclusion himself. "And, I thank you for it."

"You're most welcome." If she'd been a chicken, she'd be preening herself and strutting about now.

He said his good-bye and started for home. This day had not turned out at all like he'd expected or wanted, but its turning had set him in a new direction, one that could be for the best. A person couldn't change the way the winds blew, but he could adjust his sails.

The following week filled Stanton's thoughts with Beth Evans. She replaced Fiona with an ease that surprised Stanton, but would Beth welcome his suit? He hoped he'd be able to say and do the right things to impress her. She appeared to be a young lady with high standards, despite her crippled state. He couldn't decide how he'd arrived at that impression, but he felt sure he was right.

Should he go to the Presbyterian church again this Sunday? He feared if he did so, Beth would not allow him to walk her home. Should he go back to his church instead?

In the end, he did neither. He rode into town a little after the services had started, asked where Mr. Evans lived, and knocked on the door. He hoped Beth would be attending church, and he could talk with her father alone.

"Enter," he heard a man's faint voice call out.

He went into a very clean, small cottage. There was one big room with the kitchen and its rock fireplace to the left and a bed set up against the right wall.

Mr. Evans lay on the bed with pillows at his back to prop him up. Stanton could tell that the man had been sick, probably for a long time. He appeared gaunt with pale, wrinkled skin and white hair. His gray eyes showed signs of discomfort, but they also showed interest.

"Sir, I'm Stanton Klein, and I wanted to talk with you, if I may."

"Well, have a seat." He indicated a chair by the bed. "What can I do for you? I'm not able to do much anymore, you know." He laughed as if he hadn't a worry in the world, which couldn't be true.

"Sir, I'm going to get right to the point. I met your daughter last Sunday, and I'd like your permission to court her."

"Are you the young gentleman who walked her away from Fiona Fletcher?"

"I am. She told you about that?"

"She tells me everything, Mr. Klein." He gave a broad smile, as if he approved of Stanton's action last week. "It's been just the two of us for so long now that we're very close. Her mother died when she was eleven. Beth helped me on our farm until I fell from the barn roof and could no longer use my legs. Then we sold the farm and moved here. She manages the household and has looked after me ever since. She's a good girl, and I couldn't be more proud of her. But tell me about yourself."

Stanton told him about the farm, his wife's death, and his need for a wife. He explained his assets and told him he would be able to see his daughter well cared for.

"I can understand loneliness," Evans said when Stanton had finished. "I wouldn't have survived without Beth, and you didn't even have your child. It's also difficult to run a farm without a wife. Have you talked with Beth about this?"

Stanton squirmed in his seat. "No sir. I've only talked with her the once, and our encounter then was brief. I wanted to get your permission first."

"Well, you have it, but mine won't count for as much as Beth's. You might as well know she has a mind of her own. She has some notion in her head she won't marry unless she can find a love as strong as what my wife and I shared. Some women might consider marrying a man without a thought to his worthiness, but not Beth. She'll have to respect her husband. Although she's sweet and biddable, she has an independent streak and can be quite stubborn on rare occasions."

"Aren't those traits opposites?"

"They are, but that's my Beth. She's complex. A man would never get bored with her, and the man who wins her will be lucky indeed."

"Will you tell her you approve of my suit?"

"I will, and I'll encourage her to give you careful consideration. She's very tied to me, however. How would you propose to handle my situation, Mr. Klein?"

"Call me Stanton, please. Should Beth and I marry, we'd just move your bed and things to my house. You could join us there. The house is certainly large enough."

"I'm going to be honest with you, Stanton. I don't think I'm going to be around much longer. I feel myself getting weaker all the time. Today's been one of my better days, but the bad ones are coming more often. In a way, you may be the answer to my prayers. I've tried to hang on for Beth. I'm worried about what might happen to her after I'm gone. I'd love to see her settled with a good husband before I depart this world. You should know, however, Beth doesn't have a dowry to bring with her. We've used most of our funds on doctors, apothecary bills, and living expenses."

"I don't expect a dowry, sir. I'm just looking for the best wife I can find. I hope you're wrong, and you're around for a long time, but I appreciate your permission to court your daughter. If I'm satisfied with what I see of her, and I think I will be, I'd like to shorten the courtship and marry her before harvest season."

"We're in agreement then." He stuck out a withered hand, and Stanton shook it. "Why don't you plan to come by for dinner after church next Sunday. I'll tell Beth to cook for company."

Stanton contemplated the invitation, and then shook his head. "Let me pack my dinner and eat it in the village after church. Then I'll come by here to see her about three. I don't want to make this any harder on her than it has to be. We can have dinner together another time, when she gets to know me better."

"I like how you're already thinking about what's best for her. I feel good about all this. I'll look forward to seeing you on Sunday."

"Thank you, sir. Until Sunday then."

Stanton closed the door just as he saw the Presbyterian church letting out. He hadn't realized he and Evans had talked that long. He knew Beth would hurry home to see to her father, so he led his horse up the road. He hoped Beth wouldn't notice where he'd been. He wanted Evans to tell her first, because he felt her father would have more influence with her than he would.

He saw her walking toward him with her limp slowing her progress. She wore the same brown dress as last Sunday. He saw the moment she noticed him and slowed even more.

"Good afternoon, Miss Evans. It's wonderful to see you again. I hope you had a good church service."

"Church is always good for me, and I managed to escape today before Fiona made it out. Mistress Denny is saying you had dinner with the Fletchers. Is that true?"

He did need to get accustomed to Beth's directness, but he rather liked it over subterfuge. "Yes, her parents invited me to eat with them the first Sunday I went to your church. I went home last Sunday and have no intention of visiting with the Fletchers again." He saw a withheld question in her eyes and added, "I've found Miss Fletcher to be rather hard to take, even in small doses."

"Now, Mr. Klein, that's a harsh thing to say," she said, but her smile and the warmth in her voice overrode the censure of her words. “I would like to stay and talk more, but I must hurry home to Father.”

“Of course.” He nodded and tipped his hat. “Perhaps we can continue a conversation at some later time.”

“Perhaps.” She sounded as if she couldn’t see the possibility of that ever happening.

I hope you are wrong, Miss Evans. I hope we’ll have a long conversation next Sunday.

Beth tiptoed into the house in case her father might be resting. Instead, she found him sitting up, and he gave her a happy smile.

“If you aren’t too hungry, sit down. I had a visitor today, while you were gone.”

“Oh, who?” Beth asked as she sat down in the chair beside her father’s bed.

“Stanton Klein.”

Beth knew her mouth must have dropped open, but she couldn’t hide her surprise. “Whatever for?”

“He wanted my permission to court you.”

“I saw him as I walked home from church. He didn’t say a thing to me about it.”

“I imagine he rightly figured you’d tell him no without a moment’s thought. The man impressed me, Beth. I want you to give him a chance.”

“But, I won’t leave you, Papa. You know that.”

“Stanton said if things worked out, he’d be glad to move me to his place. I can tell he’s a good man, Beth.”

“You already have me married? I can’t believe this!”

“Now calm down, girl. I’ve done nothing of the sort. Stanton asked if he could court you, and I tried to find out what manner of man he is. He answered all my questions without any hesitation. I like him. Do you not like him?"

"I don't know him well enough to form an opinion."

"Then, when he comes calling, it will give you the opportunity to get to know him. Besides, the way you talked about him last week, I thought you might see him as your shining prince or Sir Galahad come to rescue you."

"No, I didn't think like that at all."

"You never did answer my question. Do you dislike the man, Beth?"

She gave a slight grunt of irritation. "No, I don't dislike him. He's well-mannered, and I think he may have a sense of humor. He talks as if he's more educated than many of the farmers around."

"All right, then. Get to know him better. Just give him a chance, Beth. That's all I ask. You know I love you beyond words and want the best for you. I won't be around forever, and I want to see you settled before I go. To gaze upon a grandchild would be an added blessing."

"Oh, Papa, how you do go on. Listen to you. Now you've not only got me married but with children. When am I supposed to see him? Have you planned that too?"

"He's going to come about three on Sunday afternoon. I invited him to dinner, but he declined. He said he didn't want to make it harder on you, and perhaps you would invite him later, after you two got to know each other better. He's a very perceptive and considerate man."

"Okay, you win. I'll see him Sunday afternoon, but I make no promises after that."

"Just give the man a chance, Beth. Be fair, and don't close your mind to the possibilities."

"I'll get our food. Are you hungry, Papa?"

"You know, I am a little. I do feel like eating, for a change."

The closer Sunday got, the more nervous Stanton became. He felt foolish. It had been a long time since he'd been a milk-faced boy just entering puberty. He didn't remember feeling this way when he courted Molly. Of course, if Molly hadn't accepted his proposal, he'd have just found someone else. His choices seemed more limited now, and Beth intrigued him. She seemed so different from anyone he'd ever met, and he wanted to get to know her.

It almost seemed as if Beth had somehow cast a spell on him. She never strayed far from his thoughts, and she lingered with him through whatever he did. He found himself both less lonesome due to the presence of her image and more alone for wanting to be with her. How strange was that?

At last, Sunday arrived. Stanton thought of taking Beth some of the red roses from the bush out front, but Molly had brought the cutting from her home in Philadelphia, and he wondered if it would be right to give some of the flowers to another woman. On second thought, he planned on marrying again, so why would giving the flowers be any different? Yet, the roses had just budded. None of them bloomed full, although they would do so when put into water. Why had he suddenly become so indecisive about the details? He'd never been that way before.

They'd never talked about it, but surely Molly would have understood that he'd want to remarry after her death. If he'd been the one to die first, he'd have expected her to marry again. The way he saw it, God intended for men and women to be together. That's why He made Eve for Adam.

With that in mind, Stanton cut several stems of roses and wrapped them in a newspaper.

"Going courting?" Ralph asked when he came up as Stanton mounted his horse and slipped the bottom half of the roses into a saddlebag.

"As a matter of fact, I am." Stanton took off before Ralph could ask him who. The servant didn't need to know all of Stanton's business.

Chapter Four: Courting

"If you'd be belov'd, make yourself amiable."

—Poor Richard's Almanack

"Come share dinner with us," Reverend Durk asked Stanton after the service.

"Thank you. I'd like that."

Stanton breathed a sigh of relief. He'd forgotten to pack him anything to eat, so the invitation proved fortunate indeed.

"I can't stay long," Stanton told him as they walked to the parsonage. "I have an engagement about three o'clock."

"So, are you courting now?"

"I hope I'm starting today. We'll see how it goes."

"Who's the lucky girl?"

"Beth Evans. Her father granted me permission to call, but I don't know how she feels about it. I guess I'll find out soon enough."

"Bertha and I've talked about it, and my wife thinks Beth Evans is a good woman. I trust her judgment."

"Mistress Denny also spoke highly of her, and I take that as a good sign."

"Indeed it is. I'll pray that God's will be done in the matter."

Dinner progressed in a more hectic manner than Stanton liked. The Durks had three children from ages four to twelve, and although they would eat later, they chattered and played with energy. God willing, he would be home with his wife and children at some future time.

Stanton had no nervousness or anxiety while at the Durks', but once he left, his stomach gurgled and his body stiffened. He shouldn't have eaten so much. He hoped he would settle down once he faced Beth and not be so out of kilter during their whole time together. He wondered if she felt as nervous as he did.

Reverend Durk had him leave his horse in their stable, where the animal could have hay and water. Stanton thanked him. He decided it might not be a good idea to have his horse tied in front of Beth's house yet.

He walked to Beth's home with purpose, but, once there, he hesitated. With his heart beating fast, Stanton knocked on the door. Beth opened it and smiled at him. She looked prettier than he remembered. Had she taken extra care getting ready because of his visit? He hoped so.

"Please come in and have a seat."

Two chairs were pulled fairly close to the bed, so the three of them could sit and talk. Stanton seated Beth in one and took the other for himself. Mr. Evans, although bedridden, greeted Stanton warmly.

"So you were right, Mr. Klein," Beth said.

"How so?" Stanton wondered what she meant.

"You said perhaps we'd be able to finish our conversation." Her eyes sparkled in amusement.

Stanton relaxed. She seemed to almost be laughing at the situation, and Stanton smiled at her. "Are you sorry?"

"Not in the least. I'd almost forgotten how pleasant you are to talk with."

"I'm glad you could come today, Stanton," Mr. Evans said. He appeared weaker today. "I think Beth has arranged for you to walk out back and down to the creek. There's a path you can follow."

Beth stood. "Are you sure you feel well enough to be left alone, Father?"

"Of course I do. I'm looking forward to a nap while the house is quiet."

"Okay, if you're certain."

"I am."

Stanton followed Beth out the front. If she planned for them to walk alone, without a chaperone, he would be concerned.

"Please wait here," Beth told him. "I'll be right back." She hurried to the neighbor's house and returned with two young girls who looked to be about twelve. "This is Claire and Adelle Reimer. They've agreed to come along on our walk."

Stanton didn't remember ever seeing the girls before. "Are you twins?" he asked the girls, who giggled before answering.

"No sir," Claire answered, "but we're only ten months apart."

Stanton offered Beth his arm, and he slowed his pace to hers. The girls let Beth and him get ahead, but they stayed close enough to keep the couple in sight. Beth saw him looking back.

"I told them to give us enough space to have a private conversation. I thought that might be best."

"A good idea. Do you know them well?"

"I gave them lessons in spinning, and we've spent some time together."

He liked it that she seemed so industrious. "What are some of the things you like to do, Miss Evans?"

"My, where to begin? I enjoy so many things it would be an extensive list. I loved our farm and hated to leave, but I knew we must. I miss having the land, crops, animals, and a garden. I especially liked gardening, but I like household tasks too. I love to read when I have time, and I take pleasure in a good discussion with Father, when he feels strong enough."

"Then, you wouldn't mind living out in the county on a farm?"

"No, I wouldn't mind that at all. In fact, I'd enjoy it very much. What about you, Mr. Klein? What are your pastimes when you aren't working on your farm?"

"I'm afraid I don't do much else until winter. Then, I like to read, keep up with the news, make repairs, and, on occasion, do some woodworking."

"If you don't mind me asking, what are you looking for in a wife, Mr. Stanton?"

Stanton paused. He liked Beth's directness, because it spoke of honesty and not subterfuge, but she continued to surprise him.

"I want a companion, someone to keep me from being so lonely. I need a helpmate to keep my house, and I'd like a good mother for the children I hope to have."

"How many children would you like to have?"

How should he answer? Would he scare her off if he said too many? "As many as the Good Lord sees fit to give."

"That's a good answer." She smiled.

"What about you, Miss Evans? What do you seek in a husband?"

"A godly, honest man, who'll treat me well and be a close friend. A kind man, whom I can love and respect. A man I can share everything with, and one who wants to share everything with me."

"I hope I can be that man, Miss Evans."

"In all honesty, do you think you know me well enough to propose marriage now?"

"Maybe not, but I know I like what I've seen so far. You're easy to talk with. I'm able to be myself with you and not worry about flowery speech or masking the imperfections."

She looked into his eyes as if assessing his truthfulness. "Thank you. That's the kindest thing anyone, outside of my father, has said to me in a long time. You seem sincere, and I like that about you. Now tell me about some of those imperfections."

"My wife might have said I work too hard and spend too much time out on the farm."

"I see hard work as a positive trait, and successful farming demands a lot of time."

"I keep forgetting you spent the first part of your life on a farm. It would be a blessing to have you understand."

"Did your first wife not understand?"

That Beth mentioned his first wife surprised Stanton, and she'd also discerned what he hadn't said. He would answer with as much honesty as he could. After all, he'd read somewhere that honestly could be considered the breath of one's soul.

"Molly was a good wife, and I've missed her, but she came from Philadelphia, and she never understood how much work and time a farm takes. She didn't venture far from the house, except to come to the village."

"Is your heart ready to take another wife, Mr. Klein, or will you forever be comparing the two? It's hard to compete with a memory."

He'd already given this enough thought that it didn't take him long to reply. "I assure you I'm ready for another wife, and I'll be fair. Each person has strong characteristics and weak ones. We're all different, and I don't expect a new wife to be like Molly. I want her to be herself."

"Well said, Mr. Klein, and perhaps the question should have never been asked. I've heard it's not necessary to purge someone from your heart before you can love another. The heart has the remarkable ability to expand."

Stanton looked down at his feet. Talk about the heart made him uncomfortable. He felt sure Beth would not be pleased if he told her his idea about love. How could he explain to the woman he courted that he refused to ever fall in love?

"I don't mind your questions," he told her. "In fact, I welcome any you might have."

They turned around, passed the girls, and continued their conversation on their way back to the house. Their talks were exhilarating. Beth challenged him to think in a way no one had in recent years.

"Is your name "Beth" a derivative of Elizabeth?"

"No, it's short for Bethany, which is found in the Bible."

"A place, if my memory is correct. It's unusual but pretty, just like its owner."

"It's the place where Mary, Martha, and Lazarus lived. Bethany wasn't far from Jerusalem, and it's recorded that Jesus went there several times. What about your name? Stanton is unusual too, especially for a German."

"When my grandparents came to this country, they were befriended on the trip by an Englishman with the name of Stanton. My family named me after him. I understand Stanton is also a place, although in Nottinghamshire, England. The word originally meant 'stony ground.' I guess that's appropriate considering the land I farm." He laughed at the thought of all the rocks he'd removed from his fields.

"So we both have place names. Was your mother also German?"

"She was. I take it your father is Welsh. Was your mother also?"

"Father came from Wales, but mother's family came from Germany."

"That's interesting, although it really doesn't matter to me. Molly was English and Dutch. The colonies are a mixture of people from different countries, and I rather like that." However, the thought of possibly having some German dishes set before him sounded appealing.

"You haven't mentioned my ill-shaped limb, Mr. Klein. Doesn't it bother you?"

"It doesn't bother me, but I'm concerned for you. It must make things more difficult, and I know some people have been cruel to you because of it."

"I've learned adversity can serve to make us stronger, if we have the right outlook about things."

"I'm sure you're right. Paul speaks of such things in the Bible, but, I'm afraid, many people become bitter when life delivers them trials."

"Yes, and they live miserable lives. I prefer to be happy." She smiled at him to prove her point.

"Is happiness as easy as that, Miss Evans? It seems so elusive at times."

"It's almost that easy when one has the Lord to rely upon, but what about you, Mr. Klein? You appear to be a happy person, but your statement would lead one to believe otherwise."

"I think I generally possess a happy spirit, but I've been through some of those trials in the past year. It's been a hard year for me."

"And came out stronger, I'd warrant." Her hand tightened on his arm, as if to give him her support, and he liked the feel of it. "Although, I can understand your grief at the passing of your wife."

"I hope you're right that I've come out stronger." He looked into her caring eyes and smiled.

"You've mentioned God quite often. I'm guessing He has helped you in your time of need."

Stanton looked into her face. He felt sure she deemed her faith of utmost importance. How might he answer, tell the truth, and not make her think him a heathen?

"Perhaps, but I admit I've not felt as close to God since Molly died. I've continued to go to church, but He often feels far away."

"I hope I might change that, although I'm sure grief affects people in different ways."

Stanton's heart swelled. If she hoped she could draw him closer to God that meant she planned to see him again.

"Well, here we are, back at the house."

He looked around. "Indeed we are. I'm afraid I couldn't describe to you a single thing in the landscape on our walk. I've been too captivated by my companion. You are a most interesting conversationalist, Miss Evans."

"Your words flatter me, Mr. Klein, but you always sound and look so sincere, I can find no fault in it."

"When you get to know me better, you'll find I'm honest to a fault. I meant every word I said to you."

Claire and Adelle caught up with them, and they thanked the girls for accompanying them. When Stanton turned to tell Beth good-bye, he found himself hating to leave her. Perhaps she'd allow him to see her again before next Sunday.

"Would you like to come inside for some tea and apple tarts?"

"Thank you. I couldn't pass up an apple tart. It's one of my favorites." He liked the idea of spending more time with her and was delighted she seemed to feel the same.

They went inside, greeted Beth's father, and went to the kitchen side of the room. Stanton couldn't see another room, but a ladder seemed to lead to a loft. He wondered if Beth slept up there.

Her father declined any pie or tea. Stanton and Beth sat at the table, ate, and talked like old friends. He realized how much he'd missed the pies, preserves, and all the special touches a woman brought to a home. He thought Beth must be a good cook, because he'd never had a better pie.

"Well, as much as I regret it, I must hurry and be on my way. If I don't, darkness may fall before I get home. If we were still in winter, it would already be dark."

"I hadn't realized the time. The day has passed as if it were no more than a moment."

"Indeed it has. Could I call again next Sunday?"

"Please do, and if you get into town on other days, please drop by. You're most welcome."

"Thank you. I'll do that."

On impulse, he took her hand in his and kissed the back of it before he left her. "Please think of me," he whispered as he left.

"How could I not?" he heard her whisper back.

When the door closed behind him, he stood for a moment, closed his eyes, and let the joy of the visit sink in. Beth's last comment gave him more hope than he'd had in a long time.

On Stanton's way out of the village, he saw Mr. Fletcher trying to wave him down. He stopped to see what the man wanted.

"I'm glad I caught you, Stanton," he said. "Fiona wanted me to tell you she'd be glad to accept your suit now."

Stanton stiffened in surprise. "She didn't seem too interested when I came to dinner. What changed her mind?"

"Who knows? It's been my experience that women seem to change their minds as often as their clothes. So what say you now?"

"I'm indeed honored, but please accept my regrets. I've started courting another, and it's going quite well."

"I see. I guess that's what the girl gets for dragging her feet. I'll give Fiona your regrets, then."

"Please do." Mr. Fletcher walked away, and Stanton rode on. What was that all about? Something seemed odd about Fiona's change of mind, but Stanton couldn't imagine what lay behind her invitation. However, he had no desire to pursue Fiona, not with what he'd seen of her and how well he liked Beth.

Beth stood at the door to give her heart time to flutter back where it belonged. Her whole arm grew weak and tingled after Stanton had kissed her hand, and the same feeling now rushed through her entire body. She made her way to the chair beside her father's bed and fell into it.

"So, what did you think, Daughter?"

"He seems too good to be real. He must be but a figment of my imagination."

Her father laughed. "I assure you, he's very real. So I take it, things went well."

"He seems so perfect, it scares me. I've never met anyone, other than you, I can talk to the way I can to him. I can speak my mind, and he seems enthralled with what I'm saying, makes apt comments, and appears to appreciate it all. I'm quite overwhelmed to the point I'm afraid to trust my feelings."

"Could you see yourself married to the man?"

"That's still a hard stretch at this point, but if things continue to march in the same line as they did today, I could see myself begin to consider such a thing."

"Don't be scared of marriage, Beth. Remember your mother and me. Seize such happiness for yourself. You were designed to make someone a very special wife, just as your mother did for me. Don't let fear and misgivings rob you of that. Remember, fear is not of God. Think of how many times we read 'fear not' in the Bible. That's excellent advice, Beth. Fear not."

"It seems you have made an excellent choice for me, Papa."

"I would say Stanton's the one who made the excellent choice. Remember, he's the one who came to me. He chose you first, Beth. You'll have the final say, but always remember—he chose you first."

When darkness fell, Beth went to her pallet thinking about what her father had said. Stanton had chosen to court her with the intent of making her his wife. He had chosen her over Fiona Fletcher, and that in itself was a miracle.

No man had ever paid her this much attention, and she'd never had a suitor. Cecil Shippen had flirted with her on occasion, but Cecil would flirt with any young woman, and Beth knew he'd never been serious. He just liked women. She saw him as a distant friend and nothing more.

Her thoughts turned to Stanton, and she smiled in the dark. The man moved her in a good way, but he also bothered her. Thoughts of him took her to places she'd never considered before. Could she be falling in love already? She knew she would find waiting to see him again difficult. Sunday couldn't come soon enough, and perhaps, God willing, he would call even before Sunday. Dare she hope? Or was she trying to weave the story too far ahead, before the loom had been properly strung?

Stanton couldn't believe things had gone so well with Beth or that this woman could be as congenial as she seemed. She excited him in a way no one ever had. He wondered how she felt about him. She seemed to enjoy their time together, but would she agree to marry him? Something told him she had uncommonly high standards.

When she listed the things she wanted in a husband, he found nothing that couldn't apply to him. He tried to be honest and do right, and his faith seemed to be strengthening under her influence. He'd love to be Beth's closest friend, one with whom she would share everything. He even liked the idea that she might love him. He had no problem with her loving him, but he never planned on putting himself in the same position. Yet, he could easily imagine Beth and he would do well together, have a great marriage, and form a wonderful family.

She was quite lovely, too, in her own way. She wasn't as stunning or beautiful as Fiona, but she was prettier than Molly had been.

Molly had been a full-figured woman with a round-dimpled face, but she had gained weight after their marriage. She'd never become as heavy as Mistress Denny, but she had looked plump and rounded. Her weight had never bothered him, though. He'd accepted her the way she was. He knew many qualities were more important than physical attributes, but he appreciated how Beth looked.

Chapter Five: In Middleville

"Keep thy heart with all diligence, for out of it are the issues of life."

—The New England Primer

Stanton found that Beth never left his mind, and he couldn't wait to see her again. When the leaves showed their underbellies on Tuesday morning, he knew rain might be on its way. That night the rain poured in torrents, but by Wednesday morning it had turned into a light drizzle. Telling himself the fields held too much water to work in, he saddled his horse and headed for the village.

He could have done some chores in the barn, but he left Ralph sharpening the tools instead. He had a strong urge to see Beth that he had no desire to ignore.

He felt unsure of his decision as he knocked on Beth's front door, but the smile she gave him when she opened it and saw him standing there dispelled any misgivings. She appeared happy to see him.

"Please come in. It's good to see you again."

He noticed the roses he'd brought in a vase on a shelf where they could be seen from the bed. They still looked fresh.

"It's good to see you too. I found it too wet today to do much on the farm, so I decided to use the opportunity for a quick visit."

"Not too quick, I hope. You can stay for dinner, can't you? I'm fixing a fish chowder, which won't take long to prepare."

"I'd be delighted, if it's not too much trouble. I had planned to go to the tavern to eat."

"No trouble at all. Do you frequent the tavern?"

"No, I'm not in town that often, and when I do come, it's to hear the news. I never drink much and always stick with the cider."

She smiled her approval, and then spoke. "Thank you for the roses. Father and I have both enjoyed them. I do love the sweet smell of roses. Do you play chess, Mr. Klein?"

Stanton laughed. "Let's see, I'm glad you liked the flowers, and I do play chess, but do you think you know me well enough to call me Stanton? It sounds so much less formal than Mr. Klein, which sounds much more like the way you'd address my grandfather."

"I'll call you Stanton, if you'll call me Beth."

"Now that's a deal."

She pulled out a chess set and placed it on the kitchen table. He helped her set the pieces on the board.

"Do you play often?" he asked.

"I play about once a week. It helps Father pass the time in bed."

Stanton had never played chess with a woman before, but it didn't take long for him to realize Beth excelled at the game. He forced himself to take his focus off the woman before him and concentrate on the game. He didn't want to appear an unworthy opponent. After a hard-fought battle on both sides, the game ended in stalemate.

"You're an excellent player, Stanton," she told him. "Father used to beat me most of the time, but as his health declined, he's had a harder time concentrating. I haven't had such a challenge in a long time."

"I could say the same thing. You are a formidable opponent. I can envision many long winter days spent pleasantly occupied in this manner."

He couldn't read the look Beth gave him. "Does it bother you when I speak of wanting to wed you?"

"I guess not," she answered. "It's just everything has happened at such a breakneck speed that I'm having a hard time adjusting to the idea."

"Would you prefer I didn't mention it again for a while?"

"No. I don't want you holding back anything. I want you to feel free to say whatever you think and to be honest with no hesitation."

"Good."

"Oh my. I'd better get our dinner ready. I should have started it earlier. Will you be bored to sit here and keep me company as I cook? You could always move over and talk with Father."

"I find talking with you fascinating, so I'll stay here, if I won't be in your way."

Beth looked pleased and busied herself preparing the meal. Stanton found he liked to just sit and watch her. As she stood and worked, she had a graceful way about her. It wasn't until she walked about with her limp that she became unbalanced.

Stanton watched Beth add a few carrots, diced potatoes, and onions to the pot with the fish.

"While this simmers, why don't we go tie your horse out back. There's a tub of rainwater out there, where he can drink. I'm afraid we don't have a stable."

They took care of the horse, and in about ten minutes, she stirred in butter, milk, and a little flour. She added some salt and pepper and stirred it until it came to a boil. The food smelled wonderful.

She swung the pot away from the fire and dipped some for her father first. When she had him settled with his food before him, she came back to serve theirs. Stanton wondered if they would share a trencher, but she chose two of the more modern pottery bowls and dipped chowder into them. He hoped his disappointment didn't show. He would have enjoyed sharing a trencher with her. She then set out fresh bread and butter.

The kitchen became extra warm with the fire built up enough to cook, but the cloudy weather kept it from becoming too sweltering. He took a spoonful of his chowder. It tasted as good as it smelled.

"This is delicious. I don't think I've ever eaten anything quite like it."

"Since Father has become a finicky eater, I've experimented with some recipes to try to get him to eat more. This is one of those. The fish is fresh. I just caught them this morning."

"You caught these and still managed to get back by the time I arrived?"

"When I left the house, the daylight had just begun to break through, and I only went to the creek. The fish there aren't as big as the ones sold in the markets, but I know a spot where the bigger ones stay, and I can catch enough for a meal. I filleted them into pieces to boil for the chowder.

"I didn't know you were coming, so I don't have a pie baked, but I have some fresh strawberries and sweetened cream to go on them. They're the very first of the season, and I had to search the sunny areas before the rain came to find them."

"That sounds delicious too."

"Why don't you young folks get out of here for a while?" Mr. Evans said when they'd finished their meal and Beth gathered his dish. "I'll just take a nap while you're gone."

"Would you like to walk around the village?" Beth asked him. "We can stay here, if you'd rather not. I'm sure the news of us together will spread fast."

Stanton got the feeling Beth wondered if he might be ashamed to be seen walking with her and her limp. He wanted her beside him always. Hadn't he made that clear to her?

"I have no problem with it, if you don't. Everyone will know about it soon anyway, especially if you accept my marriage proposal at some point. It seems the rain has stopped now, so we shouldn't get wet."

"You seem very sure of yourself, and I haven't heard a proposal yet." Beth didn't sound angry, but she didn't seem to be teasing, either.

Had he been too confident? He didn't feel at all certain of what Beth would do, but she had seemed to enjoy his company, and that had given him hope. Had he read more into the situation and her reactions than he should have?

"It will come. I'm trying to give you a little time to get to know me better. I felt my intentions came as quite a surprise to you."

"They did at that, but it's turned out to be a pleasant surprise. Shall we go then?"

Stanton breathed easier. She took his arm without his prodding this time, and he smiled. Things were progressing better than expected.

They strolled around the village and stopped to talk to the ones who started a conversation. Reverend Durk was working outside his house as they were passing.

"Do come in for some tea," he begged. "The missus won't forgive me if I don't bring you inside for her to have the pleasure of your company."

Beth looked around the house as they entered. She looked impressed at the roominess, much different than her small cottage.

Mistress Durk fussed over them and made them feel at home. Stanton could tell the moment Beth saw the Durks accepted her, and she relaxed. He could also tell Beth's sharp mind and knowledge of the Bible impressed the reverend. After about an hour of visiting, they took their leave. As they turned back toward Beth's cottage, they met Mistress Denny. She waddled toward them with a smile on her face.

"How wonderful to see you two together. You do make a lovely couple." She beamed. "I see you did take my advice, Mr. Klein."

Stanton looked at Beth. She didn't seem displeased at the comment, but, other than greeting the older lady, she remained quiet.

"Indeed I did, and I consider it to be some of the best advice I've ever received."

"Well, thank you. I'm glad to hear you say so. Not everyone is so disposed toward me and my advice, you know."

"If that is true, then it's their loss, madam."

"You know, you're one of my favorite people, Mr. Klein. You and Miss Evans both."

"Then we are blessed indeed."

"You've missed your calling, Stanton," Beth told him when Mistress Denny had left.

"What do you mean?"

"You're wasted here in this colonial village. You should be at court."

"No, thank you." He laughed. "I'll stick with my farm. I would be a most miserable man in anyone's court. Even Philadelphia is too cosmopolitan for me."

"What type of advice did Mistress Denny give you?"

He hesitated, unsure of how much he should tell her. "Are you sure you want to know?"

"Yes."

"It had to do with courting."

"Please be more specific. I take it the advice had something to do with me."

"It did. She told me I'd do better to pursue you than anyone else, especially Miss Fletcher."

"Mistress Denny said that? Were you considering courting Fiona?"

"Not after I saw her in action. I could never abide a person with her character, but I didn't tell Mistress Denny that. I let her believe that what she said influenced me."

"Why?"

"I guess because I see no malice in Mistress Denny. I know she spreads gossip, but I've never known her to say something untrue or try to intentionally hurt someone. I don't approve of the gossip, but there're worse people than her to have on your side."

Beth's eyes widened. "You're a complex man, Stanton, and you continue to surprise me."

"I don't think so. When you get to know me, I think you find I'm a very simple man, a simple farmer, but if you're right, we'll be well matched."

"From my perspective we'll be well matched if you are simple."

"Our first disagreement, Beth. Will we ever be able to work it out?"

She laughed. "As entertaining as you are, I think we'll work through any disagreement just fine."

Stanton realized something in that moment. He became a different man when he was with Beth. He wasn't even sure he recognized this carefree man who could joke and laugh, but he was happier than he could ever remember being, and he liked this new man better.

"I suppose I should be going, lest you become tired of my presence. I'm sure you have more to do than entertain me."

"You're wrong in that too, Stanton." Beth's eyes were dancing again. "I don't think it's possible for me to ever grow tired of you, and there's nothing I want to do more than converse with you. Come in and talk to Father for a few minutes while I take care of a chore outside. I won't be long, and I fear we've both neglected my father today."

"All right. It would be my pleasure. I like your father too." Stanton moved to the chair beside the bed.

"Stanton, how are things going?" Mr. Evans asked.

Stanton knew what he wanted to know. "Very well, sir. I have a hard time staying on the farm and getting my work done, when I want to be here with Beth. I've never met anyone like her."

"Can you tell how she feels about you?"

"No, I can't be sure how she feels, but I'm hopeful. She seems to like my company."

"That's good. Are you still of a mind to propose to her?"

"More so than ever."

Mr. Evans gave a satisfied nod. "Then do me a favor, and make that proposal the next time you have the opportunity after today."

"Is there some little thing I might bring her as a gift that would be appropriate?"

"Beth is a practical woman. She's been wishing she could make some strawberry preserves, but she's trying to stretch what's left of our funds, and she won't buy the sugar it requires. Bring her a cone of sugar."

"All right. Thank you."

Beth's returned ended more talk in this vein. "Can you stay for supper, Stanton?"

"I'd better not, for I need to get back to the farm before dark, and I have an errand to run. Would it be okay if I leave and take care of my business, and then return for a few minutes and say good-bye before I leave for home?"

"Of course."

Stanton went straight to the merchant's. He bought himself some tea and the sugar for Beth. He also bought her a handkerchief with lace trim. He would save it and present it to her on Sunday.

When he came out, he saw Fiona walking with Cecil. She giggled over something he said and pulled on his arm so he moved closer to her. Stanton knew he'd done the right thing to avoid Fiona Fletcher, and he regretted he'd even considered her at all.

"I decided to get you a little something when I went to the store." he told Beth when she opened the door to him. He handed her the sugar.

Beth appeared surprised and speechless for a moment. "You shouldn't have bought anything for me. Is this why you went?"

"No, I needed some tea, but please accept my small attempt to give you something you might need."

"The roses were plenty, Stanton. I don't feel right accepting gifts you buy."

"Make some strawberry preserves or something, and perhaps we can enjoy them together this winter. If not, you can divide them with me. I'm afraid I no longer have any preserves or pickles put back."

"All right. As long as one way or another half of the jam will be yours."

"May I call on you again Sunday? Would you like to attend my church, should I come to yours again, or would you prefer I wait and come by here after church?"

"What would you prefer?"

"Why don't you come with me? You seemed to like the Durks, and I know they liked you. In addition, should we marry, we'll need to make a decision about which church we'll attend."

"All right."

"I'll be by to pick you up before church Sunday morning, then. I'll bring the wagon, and perhaps we can go for a ride in the afternoon, if we can find a chaperone."

Stanton rode home thinking about how he might propose Sunday. He wondered why Mr. Evans wanted him to propose right away, but that suited Stanton fine. He didn't want Beth to feel pressured or rushed, but from his perspective, the sooner the better. He couldn't wait to take Beth home, to have her with him all the time. Even spending the whole day with her wasn't enough. He already missed her.

Chapter Six: The Proposal

"Who can find a virtuous woman? for her price is far above rubies."

—Proverbs 31:10

"Beth, could I have a word with you?" her father said as soon as Stanton had left.

She sat down beside his bed and waited for him to collect his thoughts. She could tell this hadn't been one of his best days, but he'd spent most of it sleeping, so he'd at least gotten some rest.

"How do you feel about Stanton?"

She paused a long time to consider her answer. "I like him. In fact, I've seen nothing I don't like as yet. He's witty, charming, and considerate. He's been a most pleasant surprise."

"Are you considering him as a husband?"

Beth looked at her father. When he began his questioning like this, he intended to teach her something or point her in the right direction.

"I guess I am, but I don't think I'm ready to make such an important decision this soon. I've only known him a week, Papa."

"But you've spent more hours with him than many people who've courted a month."

"A month is still a short time when it comes to courting."

"Perhaps, but some people have arranged marriages and never court or get acquainted with their mates until after the marriage. In fact, for most people, marriage is a business proposition to gain children, property, or money."

"Maybe so, but that would never be agreeable with me. You know this."

"I think I may have spoiled you in this area, Beth. Perhaps I did you a disservice by telling you of the love your mother and I shared. I set you to dreaming dreams and having high expectations where marriage is concerned. Let me ask you something. Do you think you'll feel any more certain about what you want to do in two or three months?"

"I don't know. Perhaps."

"Be truthful with yourself, Beth."

"I guess not. I do miss him when he's gone and wish we were together again."

"That should tell you much. Don't be afraid to go out on a limb once in a while, sweetheart, because that's often where the best fruit grows. Can you see yourself spending the rest of your life with him better than you can any other man, even one of your dreams?"

I think he has become the man of my dreams. "Yes, I think I can."

"Then do me a favor and say yes as soon as he proposes."

"Okay. If it's important to you, I'll say yes and marry Stanton Klein, if and when he asks me."

"Good, good." He patted her hand. "Now if you'll take out a pillow or two from behind my head, I'm tired and would like to rest some more."

She did as he asked and kissed his cheek. "I love you, Papa."

"I love you too, Beth, and I just want to see you happy."

"I know, Papa."

Beth went to the kitchen and began preparing supper. She smiled at the cone of sugar sitting on the table. How had Stanton known she needed sugar? Sometimes she thought the man could almost read her mind. She wished she could read his. What did he truly think of her? Would he ask her to be his wife, as he'd indicated? She could scarce believe it.

Besides being quite wonderful, he was such a handsome man. He stood tall, with blond hair, blue eyes, and a light tan from his time in the sun. He could have any woman around, so why had he chosen her, a cripple?

His classic good looks could put him in the role of a prince with ease. She smiled to herself. He even had the court manners to go with it, but she shouldn't be thinking about Stanton like some silly schoolgirl.

Stanton's image became stubborn, however, and refused to move from her thoughts. She must have thought of him more than a hundred times a day, and the nights brought no respite. He filled her dreams. Was she in love? She couldn't believe it. A person couldn't fall in love in a few days, could she?

Sunday came with the promise of a bright day. Beth got up early and took her time washing and dressing.

She had three good dresses she'd made. She'd made the light-brown homespun from all the same color, but she could wear her white tucker around the neckline for an accent. The deep-gold one had a lighter-gold stomacher and outer petticoat. The other was a deep green trimmed with beige lace.

Stanton had seen her in the brown more than any other, so today she chose the green. If she got married soon, she'd wear the gold, because she'd made it last, and it had more details.

Although Stanton came a little early, Beth had already changed and sat waiting for him. Her heart gave a jump when she heard his knock, and it raced as she opened the door to his smile. She offered him a cup of tea and drank one with him before they headed for church.

Everyone at church welcomed them, and Beth could tell Stanton was well liked. The Durks came over with a special greeting.

"Come sit with me, when you get ready to take a seat," Mistress Durk said. "The women and men sit on different sides here."

"Oh, Stanton, darling." An attractive strawberry-blond woman came up to Stanton and put her hand on his arm. "I hoped you'd be here today. We need to get together again soon."

Beth looked in surprise at her forwardness. The woman presented herself well, but she looked as if she were approaching middle age. As she stared, Beth could see evidence the woman used some cosmetics to enhance her face.

"I don't think so, Mistress Knotts. May I present Beth Evans? Beth this is the widow Agnes Knotts."

"Pleased to meet you, Mistress Knotts."

"*Wellll* now. Oh my," the widow sputtered. "Are you two together?"

"Yes, madam. Beth and her father have granted me the honor of calling on Beth."

"You must like the young ones who are just out of school, Stanton."

"No, I like a pleasant, responsible, mature woman who has enough poise and self-respect not to run after men."

"I thought we had something." She looked at Stanton and turned red, as the meaning of what he'd just said sank in. With a loud huff, she flounced off.

"I didn't," Stanton muttered as she left.

Beth looked at Stanton wondering what had just taken place and if he and the widow had had some sort of connection. He didn't seem the type of man who would toy with two women at the same time, but what did she really know of Stanton Klein?

He caught her look. "I'm sorry about that, Beth. The woman has pursued me since Molly died, and she won't give up. I promise you I have done my best to discourage her, but she has been relentless."

"Have you been to her house?"

"Never."

"Has she been to your house?"

"Only to bring food in the company of other women. If I wanted the widow, I could have her, Beth, but she's too forward-acting for my taste. You know who I want, and I'm pleased with my choice."

She looked into his eyes, and they spoke of sincerity. "I believe you," Beth whispered just before he led her to the bench with Mistress Durk and seated her. The smile he gave her and the warmth in his eyes almost stole her breath.

The Lutheran service included more formal ceremony than the Presbyterian, but Beth had no problem following along. There were some parts that were similar.

The Durks invited them to dinner afterward, but Beth told them she needed to go home to see about her father. He seemed to be getting weaker.

They entered the house to the smell of food. She'd prepared a roast earlier, so she sliced it and the bread and served a pot of different vegetables cooked together. The day had turned warm enough that most of the food would be fine at room temperature.

"Are we going to be able to go for a ride?" Stanton asked her.

"I'm to fetch Adelle to sit with Father while we're gone, and Claire will ride with us."

"Where would you like to go? Would you like to see my farm?"

"I would love to, but we'd better save that for another time. With Father not feeling well, I don't want to leave him for long. You choose a place."

Stanton helped Beth into the middle of the wagon seat and put Claire on the outside. Then he went around and climbed into the driver's seat beside Beth. His body brushed against hers as he drove the wagon, and she became very aware of him. She couldn't decide if the tingling it invoked felt good or not. It certainly felt unsettling.

The day had turned almost too warm, but a slight breeze helped cool her. They rode for about thirty minutes before Stanton pulled the wagon off the road in a flat area under a shade tree. He set the brake and got out.

"Why don't you stay with the wagon, Claire?" he said. "Beth and I are going down to that log by the river, but we'll stay within sight."

Claire nodded, and Stanton lifted Beth down. His hands encircled most of her waist, and he set her down as if she weighed no more than a pillow. She felt light-headed by the time she had her feet on the ground.

To help Beth through the loose rocks on the way down, Stanton took her left hand in his left, and put his right arm around her back just above her waist to steady her. She thought about protesting, but her leg often caused her to lose her balance on uneven ground, so she said nothing.

When they got to the log, they stood in front of it and watched the river flow. Stanton didn't remove his hands from her, but she felt so secure with his arm around her, she again said nothing.

"Life is a lot like a river, isn't it?" she said. "They both keep moving along, changing things with their flow."

"I like to listen to a river," Stanton said. "It seems to sing of keeping to a task, of never giving up."

"Perhaps you're a lot like that river—constant, reliable, persevering, garnering respect wherever you go."

He raised an eyebrow but said nothing until he seated her on the log and sat down beside her. He picked up her hand again, and rubbed the top of it with his thumb. "Is that how you see me, Beth?"

"I see that and more. Every time we're together, I see something else I like."

"Then won't you marry me, Beth, so we can stay together? I don't want to keep saying good-bye and not seeing you for days. I want you with me always. Make me happy and say you'll be my wife."

Beth sucked in a deep breath. She remembered she'd told her father that she would accept, when Stanton asked, but this had come sooner than she expected. Was she ready?

She looked at Stanton again. His expectant face had turned to pleading, as he waited for her response. She recalled his care, his easy manner, and how much she respected him. The fact that she loved him washed over her.

"Yes."

"What did you say?"

"Yes, I'll marry you and be your wife."

For a second, he looked as if he didn't believe what he'd heard. Then he stood and pulled her into an embrace. Being in his arms felt so right, she could have stayed there for hours. She rested her head on his shoulder and marveled at how he felt and smelled. Could he feel how fast her heart beat? Could she even stand, if he let go?

"Wonderful! Thank you, darling. I'll make sure you never regret it." He sounded ecstatic right before he kissed her on the cheek. She pulled back enough to look at him. His face radiated happiness.

"Come." He guided her toward the wagon. "Let's tell Claire what just happen, so she doesn't get the wrong idea, and we should go let your father know. I'll post the banns tomorrow morning. How soon can we wed?"

Beth loved the enthusiasm she heard in his voice. "You tell me." She liked teasing him.

"What about two weeks from tomorrow? I think the banns have to be posted for at least two weeks in our county." His exuberance reminded her of a young boy.

"Okay, in two weeks."

Although he acted as if he'd just been granted his heart's desire, he hadn't said he loved her. He must, however, if his actions were any indication.

Her father perked up some when he heard their news. “This is good,” he said as he reached for Beth’s hand. “You’ve made the right decision, Beth.”

“Where do you want to get married?” Stanton asked her. “I’ll speak to the preacher tomorrow too.”

“I believe it’s customary to get married in the woman’s church,” her father told Stanton.

Stanton nodded. “That’s fine. I’ll speak with your minister and reserve the church. Will you have attendants?”

Beth thought about that. With a bit of sadness, she realized she had no friends close enough to ask. She shook her head.

“I’ll just come from a front bench like you will, Stanton.”

“I’ve been dreaming of watching you walk down the aisle, Beth,” her father said with his eyes growing watery. “I’m sorry I can’t walk you down to present you to Stanton, but I do plan to be there. Walk down the aisle for me, so I can see you.”

“I’d like to see you coming to me from across the church too, Beth,” Stanton added, “but if you don’t feel comfortable doing so, I’ll understand.”

Beth dreaded being on display for others to gawk at. Did she dare try to walk down the aisle? Yes, she wouldn’t be that selfish. She’d do anything she could for these two men. “How can I refuse the two of you? I’ll walk down the aisle, if I don’t trip along the way.”

Beth saw Stanton on Monday. He dropped by to tell them the banns had been posted, and would be read Sunday. He’d scheduled the church and preacher for a three o’clock wedding in two weeks.

"Is it permissible for Beth and me to go for a brief walk alone, since we're now officially engaged?" Stanton asked Beth's father.

"I think that's allowed. In fact, I think that's a good idea. Could I also ask a favor of you, Stanton?"

"Of course, sir."

"Would you work it out to get me to church for the wedding? I can sit in a chair if I'm helped into it."

"I'll be glad to. Now, I'm going to take Beth for that walk."

Stanton led Beth down to the creek. "Is there anything you need for the wedding, Beth?"

"No, you've already done enough."

"I'll be providing for you for the rest of our lives, so it might as well start now."

"I hope I'll be contributing to the farm and our lives together too."

"You will, darling. I didn't mean to make it sound otherwise. I just want our wedding to be special for you. I hope it will be all that you want."

"Being wed to you will make it special, Stanton."

Beside the brook, he pulled her into his arms and kissed her. At first, his lips were soft and tender, but she felt the kiss grab at her heart and travel all the way to her toes. As she relaxed in his embrace and responded to his kiss, it intensified, until Beth knew she wouldn't still be upright without his arms supporting her.

He pulled his lips away but still held her. "I've wanted to kiss you from the first time I came to see you, but we'd better head back. Another one of those, and I'm not sure I could control myself. I'm glad the wedding isn't far off. I can't wait to have you for my wife."

Beth hated to pull apart, but she knew he was right. She had never felt so drawn to someone in a physical way like this before.

He put his arm around her waist to lead her back. Beth still struggled with some of the emotions she'd felt in that kiss. They were all new to her, and she didn't know what to make of them.

"Are you all right?" he asked when she hadn't said anything. "I didn't hurt you, did I?" Concern showed on his face.

"No, I'm fine. Your kiss just left me as weak as pauper's tea."

He smiled. "It affected me too, but I hope you liked it."

"Too much, I'm afraid." She laughed to ease the tension building in her.

He squeezed her waist. "You make me happier than I've ever been before, Beth."

"Do you mean it? Ever?"

"Ever. At any time in my life."

"I'm glad."

On Tuesday afternoon, Beth heard a knock on the door. Thinking she would find Stanton on the other side, she rushed to open it, but the Durks stood there. She pushed down her disappointment, invited them in, and introduced them to her father.

"Stanton came to see us yesterday," Reverend Durk said. "We talked about your upcoming wedding, and Bertha and I wanted to volunteer to help. Stanton is a special friend, and we were impressed with you too. I wondered if you would do me the honor of allowing me to walk you down the aisle in lieu of your father."

Beth looked into the kind eyes. "I would like that. You can help keep me from tripping or making a fool of myself. Thank you."

"And I asked Stanton if I could organize some refreshments and perhaps some music afterward for your guests," Mistress Durk said. "Stanton told me I should speak to you about it. What do you say? I'd like to do this for you and Stanton."

"How can I refuse such a generous offer? Thank you."

"That's very kind of you," her father told them. "I know Beth has been concerned, and this will make things easier for her."

The Durks stayed for a little while and then left. Beth's small wedding plans seemed to be expanding. At least by having it at three o'clock on a Monday, there shouldn't be a large crowd there.

Chapter Seven: Interlude

"Courage would fight, but Discretion won't let him."

—Poor Richard's Almanack

"I have something I want to show you, Beth. Go into the trunk stored in the corner of the loft and bring the package tied in a sheet."

Beth did as her father requested. She'd forgotten about the trunk, but when she opened it, she realized it contained some of her mother's things.

"Open it," her father said when she presented him the parcel.

She found a beautiful silk dress in a deep pastel green trimmed in ivory accents, and there were ivory slippers to match. It seemed a little out of style, but it still retained its elegance.

"This was your mother's wedding dress. You're about the same size, and I thought you might want to refurbish it to wear for your wedding. In fact, take anything you want from the trunk. Your mother would have wanted you to have them."

"Thank you, Papa." Beth couldn't get any more out than that. A flood of emotions overwhelmed her. She turned and headed back to the loft, so her father wouldn't see her tears.

Beth spent most of the afternoon rummaging through the trunk. There were several dresses she would take with her to alter when she had time. The fabrics were nice. A new bed gown of fine lawn that she could use for her wedding night lay among the other garments. All hers were quite worn, and none were made of fabric this fine. She also found some cloth, undergarments, and a cloak.

She held the gown and ran her hand over it, imagining wearing it for Stanton. The thought both thrilled her and terrified her at the same time. *Lord, help me to be the wife he needs.*

Beth didn't see Stanton again all week. She spent the latter half of the week worrying and filled with doubts. Why hadn't he come to see her midweek? Had his thrill been all in the pursuit, and now his ardor had cooled?

She dressed with care Sunday morning. If Stanton didn't come to see her before church, maybe he would come to her church, or, at the very least, he should come after church. She felt certain she would see him sometime today.

Since she had her mother's silk for the wedding, she decided to wear her gold dress. She liked the way it fit, and the color suited her. The gold made her skin look flawless, her eyes the color of emeralds, and her dark hair shine with highlights.

When the knock on the door came, her heart jumped for joy. She knew who it had to be, so she ran to bid him enter. He looked so happy to see her, all her doubts disappeared.

She ushered Stanton into the house, and he pulled her into a hug and kissed her forehead. He took liberties now that they were betrothed, but she didn't chide him for it. She enjoyed those liberties too much herself.

"I've missed you dearly," he whispered into her hair before he let her go.

In that moment, all her misgivings fled. It felt so good to be in his arms. The gentleness of his touch soothed her. She felt cherished.

He pulled back, gave a sigh, and slid the back of his hand down her cheek, as if he couldn't get enough of her. Would he always show this much affection?

"You look so lovely today," he told her. "I like that dress."

"Thank you."

He pulled a roll of ivory lace from his pocket. "Here, I brought you this. It's the last lace my grandmother made before she died."

She looked at the delicate lace and thought about all the hours that must have gone into it. "It's beautiful, and it matches the dress I'll wear for our wedding. I'll add it to the dress tomorrow. Thank you, but you don't have to give me something every time you come."

"I haven't. I didn't give you anything on Monday." He seemed to hold back his laughter and his eyes sparkled.

Beth wondered why he hadn't already given the lace to Molly, but she dared not ask. It pleased her that he'd come for her before church.

"You gave me a kiss," she whispered, so her father wouldn't hear.

"Soon you can have those anytime you'd like."

"Are you certain? I can just see me running across the field after the plow to claim a kiss."

Beth felt her face grow warm. How brazen he must think her, and he'd already said he didn't like forward women.

He chuckled. "You don't know how delighted that statement makes me. You excite me beyond words, Beth. I suspect this week is going to be the longest one of my life."

"Are we going to church together today?" she asked as she led him to the kitchen. They had time for a cup of tea, and talk flowed around the table.

"Since you attended church with me last Sunday, I thought we might go to yours today, but soon we'll need to decide which one we want to attend after we're wed. Which would you prefer?"

Beth sat back in surprise. Was he allowing her to choose?

"I like the services and preaching better at mine," she told him, "but I admire Reverend and Mistress Durk, so you choose."

"We still have time to think about it. The decision doesn't have to be made today."

Stanton tied his horse in the back of her house, and they walked to church. As they approached, Beth saw Fiona talking with her usual group of girls.

"Can you believe he's marrying her and him so handsome? She must have bewitched the poor man somehow." The girls' eyes widened.

"Besides that," Fiona continued, "her actual name is Bethany. That's a Hebrew name, so she must be a Jew." Beth stiffened at the intended barb.

Stanton put his free hand over hers resting in his arm. "I can't believe the viciousness of some of the young women today," he said loud enough to be heard. "Do you know that some of them stand outside the church and slander others? In most colonies, slander is not only a sin but a punishable crime as well."

Most of the other girls took a step back. Fiona turned to face Stanton and Beth.

"Miss Fletcher," Stanton continued, "I couldn't help but hear your comment. I believe your mother's given name is Mary, a name also found often in the Bible and Hebrew in origin. Does that make your mother a Jew? Furthermore, what would be wrong if Beth did have Jewish heritage? Jesus was a Jew."

Fiona stood frozen as if she were in shock. Then she gave a little fling of her head and marched off.

Stanton patted Beth's hand before he took his away. "I'm sorry that happened. Miss Fletcher spoils her attractiveness with her mean spirit."

"Thank you for defending me."

"Always, dear."

The other girls had scattered. Beth looked at Stanton in awe. He would have made a very good knight in shining armor.

The day raced away faster than the winged Nike in Greek mythology. After church, Beth served dinner. Her father napped on and off during most of the day, and she and Stanton played a game of chess, which she won.

Stanton wrinkled his brow. "I don't think I had my mind on the game today," Stanton said, "so you had me at an unfair advantage."

"Oh, and where had your mind gone?"

She expected him to say on the wedding, but he surprised her by saying, "Walk with me to the creek, and I'll show you."

She knew exactly what he meant, then, and wondered if her face had reddened. She could feel her blood racing as she got up. However, she looked forward to another kiss as much as he did. They walked down to the creek hand in hand.

"I'll try to come back into town during the middle of the week, but I'm not sure if I'll be able to. Unexpected events kept springing up all last week. Just when I thought I might have made it in, something else came up. In addition, I have some cleaning out to do."

"Don't worry about cleaning, Stanton. I can do that."

"I'm sorting through some things and discarding those not needed."

Beth realized he must be talking about cleaning out Molly's things. She marveled at his thoughtfulness and prayed she could be the wife he deserved.

"Come here," he said.

He pulled her into his arms and began teasing her lips with his. She leaned into his embrace, and he kissed her in earnest. Not thinking about anything but the kiss and the tautness at strange places in her body, she molded herself to him and returned his kiss.

She had no idea how long the kiss lasted, but it ended all too soon. She had become too breathless to speak, but Stanton didn't seem to have that problem.

"I could get lost in kissing you," he said. "You are amazing. Have you never been kissed before?"

"Not like this. Not by anyone other than my parents." Did he see her as experienced in such things? "I've simply followed your lead."

"Like I said—'amazing.'"

Stanton rode back to the farm lost in thought. He had said it right. Beth was amazing. That she enjoyed kissing gave him an unexpected gift. Molly hadn't. Oh, she hadn't minded a kiss on the cheek or a quick peck on the lips, but she'd never wanted a passionate kiss like Beth allowed. Allowed? Beth had also kissed him back.

What had she said? She'd been following his lead, which meant she would permit him to teach her. He wondered how much she knew about the physical side of marriage. Not much, he'd warrant, since her mother died when she was eleven. He'd have to be gentle and woo her with care. He certainly didn't want to frighten her.

He wondered now how he'd ever been happy with Molly, but he hadn't realized what he'd been missing then. He'd taken their marriage stoically and accepted things as they were. Perhaps he'd even been glad Molly had not turned out to be a threat to his heart. He'd assumed wives wouldn't be as demonstrative as a loose woman, and he had no intention of associating with them. He had done that as he'd moved into adulthood, but that period of his life left bad memories. He knew better now.

Was Beth a threat to his heart? She could be, but being aware of the potential, he could make sure he'd never love her. Care for her, yes, but never love her with such intensity she became the most important thing in his life. He would never be like his father. He would not set himself up for that kind of pain and, in grief, be willing to leave those who depended on him.

Stanton's week turned out to be as busy as he feared it might. Cleaning out Molly's things took much longer than he'd expected. He packed up most of them to take to the Durks. Mistress Durk might choose to use some of the things, and the rest could be given to the poor.

The farm also required his attention. The cow had trouble birthing and required an all-night vigil. Stanton found himself so tired the next day, he did only what had to be done and went to bed early. Then, a fox tried to get into the chickens just after Stanton had fallen asleep, and he had to get up to chase him away. In the dim waning light, the wily creature paused just before he darted away with a chicken in his mouth. The animal looked straight at Stanton and appeared to grin. Stanton tried not to believe in luck, but he hoped this didn't prove to be a bad omen. Ralph later said he hadn't heard any of the commotion.

Then, raccoons began getting into his corn, and he tried to get out to the field before dawn to shoot them, or at least to run them away. They seemed to multiply, as he got rid of them. For every one he shot, two would return.

Ralph hadn't done as much as Stanton expected, and so Stanton spent much of the week doing things that had been left undone. If he worked alongside Ralph, the man seemed to work fine, but if he left, Ralph slackened. Stanton wanted things in fair order when Beth first saw the farm, because he wanted her first impression to be a good one.

Thursday came before he managed to go to Middleville. He left as early as possible and drove the wagon to the Durks' to drop off Molly's things first. The day promised to be another warm one.

He didn't stay long to visit at the Durks'. When he finished unloading, he hurried to make the stops necessary to arrange to transport Mr. Evans to the church on Monday. He'd also decided to rent a carriage for the wedding.

After taking care of all his business, the noon hour neared when he knocked on the door at the Evanses' home. Mr. Evans called for him to enter, and disappointment fell on Stanton like nighttime in a forest. Beth must not be here.

"She went to the store," Mr. Evans informed him.

"I'll go there and see if she needs any help with her things. I brought the wagon today."

Upon arriving in the business section, he parked the wagon, got out, and started for the store. He saw Beth before she saw him. She seemed to be having a serious conversation with Cecil Shippen in front of the store. He stopped when he caught some of the words and stepped to the side to stand in the shadow of a tree and blend in with its trunk.

"Ah, Beth, why would you attach yourself to a man so much older? You know my feelings for you."

"Stanton isn't so much older, and, no, I don't know how you feel about me. I thought you were interested in Fiona."

"No, I'd say Fiona is interested in me. Haven't I come to your aid time and time again, even against Fiona's sharp tongue?"

"I appreciate those times, Cecil, but I'm quite happy with my choice for a husband."

"You don't know what you're missing. There's not a young woman in the whole colony who wouldn't be glad to have my attentions directed toward her."

"And I'm sure there aren't many who haven't had your attentions."

"Ah, Beth, you wound me. What have I done to warrant such a low regard for me? You do me a grave injustice."

Beth gave a soft laugh. "We've been friends since we were in dame school. I like you as a friend, but that's all. Without a doubt, Stanton is the man for me."

"I won't take kindly to you rejecting me for Stanton Klein." Cecil's light, teasing tone had vanished. "You either meet me behind your house tonight, or there'll be no friendship."

"I'm sorry to hear that, Cecil, but you know I'm not that sort of woman. I would never meet a man without a chaperone, and I have no intentions of going out at night."

"You need to experience a moment of freedom before you wed. Meet me, Beth. You won't be sorry."

"I'm already sorry you asked such a thing. Please take care, Cecil. I hope you won't hold me in ill regard, but what you ask of me is impossible. I'm getting married on Monday."

When Beth turned to walk away, Stanton saw her eyes fall on him beneath the tree. He stepped out to meet her.

Chapter Eight: The Wedding

"Keep your eyes wide open before marriage, half shut afterwards."

— Poor Richard's Almanack

"Why didn't you make yourself known? Are you spying on me?" Beth looked at him with disbelief written on her face.

He took the packages she carried. "When I called at you house, your father said you were here, so I came to see if you needed help carrying your purchases. I heard Cecil trying to talk you out of marrying me, and I stopped short. I'm sorry I ended up eavesdropping. I should have rushed forward and rescued you. I should have punched the reprobate."

"He's harmless, Stanton, and you have no need to worry about Cecil and me." She placed her hand on his arm to reassure him. "I know what he's like. He can be charming at times, but he uses it to his advantage. His mission in life is to chase women, so I know better than to give him serious thought. I pray that he'll change and settle down, because he's wasting his life away, but he's never been the man for me, nor would he ever be. If I dared succumb to his advances, he'd soon be through with me. It's winning the prize that means more to him, and once he has it, he moves on in pursuit of another."

It made him happy to hear her words, but they didn't dispel the emotions raging within. He should have attacked the rogue. How dare the man make Beth such a reprehensible offer! How dare he make an effort to seduce Stanton's soon-to-be wife.

"Sometimes a man gets hurt when a woman rejects him, and he wants the woman worse than he would have if she hadn't jilted him," he told Beth. "It's human nature to want what we can't have. I don't like the man, and I don't trust him."

He set her packages in the wagon and helped her onto the seat. When he sat beside her, she continued their conversation as he drove at a snail's pace so he could hear her well.

"Please don't be jealous. Jealousy can be like troublesome weeds. If not stopped, they multiply and choke out all the good plants. Don't let Cecil ruin our time together. I'm so happy to see you. When you didn't come yesterday, I feared I'd have to wait until Sunday."

Jealous? Was he jealous? He'd never been jealous before in his life, but Beth could be right. Anger and perhaps jealousy. It also rankled him that she called the man Cecil and not Mr. Shippen, but he needed to get control of himself, or else his anger would put him in a bad light.

"I'm not sure I'm jealous, but the way Cecil behaves with women does make me angry."

She looked at him with a softer face. "If you allow someone to make you angry, then you're letting him control you. But can't we just forget about Cecil for now and enjoy our time together?" The plea in her expression touched his heart.

"You're right. We shouldn't let Cecil spoil our day. Thank you for telling him that I'm the man for you. I hope that's how you truly feel. I know our courtship has been brief, but I hope you have no qualms about our marriage on Monday."

"I recognize how well suited we are every time we're together. The nervousness I have about the wedding has more to do with me being the center of attention at the ceremony and the unknown aspects of being a wife. I don't want you to be disappointed in your choice."

"If only you could know how deep my regard for you is. With the way I feel about you, I can promise I'll not be disappointed. I'm sure everything will be well with us. What has you the most concerned?"

She blushed, and he knew. "Does it have to do with our wedding night?"

She gave an almost imperceptible nod. "You've been married before, but I have almost no idea of what you'll expect of me." Her face turned an even darker shade of red.

"Please don't be concerned, darling. Remember how you said you didn't know how to kiss, but you let me guide you. I'll do the same here. There's nothing required of you but to be willing."

She nodded again, but he knew he should change the topic of conversation. He didn't want to make her uncomfortable. How remarkable they were able to have such an intimate talk at all. At least she'd been honest with him, even about this difficult, personal subject.

"Things at the farm have been busy," he told her. "I've been torn between wanting to see you and needing to get things done there. My bondsman works fine as long as I'm there to watch, but he does little when I'm gone."

"I didn't know you had a servant."

"I had to have someone to help in the fields. I've been wondering if I shouldn't also get a woman to help you in the house. What do you think?"

"I can't see that would be necessary—not at first anyway. Perhaps when we have children."

Children. Stanton smiled. It sounded as if Beth looked forward to having children too. He couldn't wait. What he wouldn't give for a healthy son!

"We'll wait and see, then, but let me know if you'd like to have someone."

Beth looked uncomfortable, as if she didn't want to be pressed on the issue. Stanton didn't understand why she wouldn't be pleased that he wanted to make things easier for her, but he let the topic drop for now.

"I have my dress ready. The lace you gave me added just the right touch. I hope you'll think I look nice in it." She looked away, almost embarrassed by her need for reassurance.

"I'll think you're lovely. I need to ask your advice about something, though. I have a wig, but I don't wear it often. I agree with Benjamin Franklin that wigs are too uncomfortable, especially in hot weather, but I want to please you, and I wouldn't mind to wear it for our wedding. What do you think?"

"I like your hair." She hesitated, then reached up and touched a lock. "It's soft and thick. I'd prefer you without a powdered wig."

"That's how it will be, then."

The day in late June went by at record speed. It became so hot, Beth didn't plan to cook, but they had cheese, beef, bread, and fruit for dinner. Her father napped most of the time, but when he woke, they talked about tomorrow, and Stanton told them of the plans he'd made.

"I have some men who will come by and help get you first, Mr. Evans. I have a special chair with armrests for you, and they will set you and the chair in the wagon and then carry you both into the church. I've rented a carriage and a driver for Beth. Reverend and Mistress Durk will come to get her in it and accompany her to the church."

"I can walk to the church," Beth said. "It's too close for a carriage ride."

"Not for your wedding. You and I will also use it to go to my farm afterward. I've hired Mistress Denny to see to your father's supper, and Ralph will stay with him through the night. We'll return the carriage on Tuesday morning and load the wagon with the things you want to move to the farm. We'll take your father with us. In the meantime, you can pack a bag with the things you'll need for Monday night and put it in the carriage when the Durks pick you up."

"It sounds as if you have everything well planned out," Beth said. Stanton couldn't tell if the fact pleased or irritated her.

"I appreciate you doing all this," Mr. Evans said. "With Beth's mother gone and me incapacitated, you've been a real blessing."

"My pleasure."

Stanton didn't stay for supper. He told them he wanted to get his evening chores done before dark and retire. He felt tired enough; he just hoped he could sleep. The excitement for Monday had been building.

When Beth walked him to the door, he pulled her against the wall and out of Mr. Evans's sight. He gave her a long, passionate kiss and hoped it would help ease her fears.

"Everything will be fine between us, Beth," he told her when he had enough breath back to speak. "I think we were meant for each other."

Stanton had no misgivings about marrying Beth. He knew he'd made the right choice. Everything looked so promising he couldn't wait until they were husband and wife.

He couldn't tell what caused the difference this time. Doubts had plagued him the night before he wed Molly. He'd been younger then, and that made it harder for him to know his own mind. Beth seemed so different too. He already felt a connection with her he'd never felt with Molly.

As he neared the farm, Stanton's mind moved to the incident with Cecil and Beth. Cecil had better make himself scarce, or Stanton didn't think he'd be able to control himself. He wanted to beat the rascal senseless. He might not have misgivings about marrying Beth, but he had plenty about Cecil Shippen. He hoped the man had sense enough to stay out of his sight, but from all Stanton had seen, the man didn't.

On Sunday, Stanton took Beth to his church again. That way he didn't have to see Cecil, and they'd gone to the Presbyterian church the previous Sunday. The afternoon sped by, as it always did when he was in Beth's company. "Tomorrow," he kept telling himself. After tomorrow there'd be no more good-byes.

Stanton awoke early Monday morning, and it seemed as if time refused to budge. He should have scheduled the wedding for ten o'clock in the morning. Waiting until afternoon would be torturous.

He dressed with care, had Ralph hitch up the wagon, and they drove to Middleville. This morning felt a little cooler than recent ones, and Stanton hoped it meant the day would also be more comfortable. He knew Mistress Durk planned to serve the refreshments and have music and dancing outside. Rain would be disastrous.

At least the Puritan influence hadn't completely banned dancing in all the colonies. Although some people in Pennsylvania considered dancing to be wrong, many in the colony viewed it as an acceptable social function. He hoped he could lead Beth in a dance and hold her in his arms to show all those attending she belonged to him.

He worried about how Beth would feel about the dancing. He knew her to be sensitive about her limp and being the center of attention. He knew she would never be able to move through a minuet, a reel, or a country dance, but he hoped he could coax her into a simple waltz. Not many people around Middleville had heard of the slow dance, but he knew of it. People in Austria and southern Germany had been dancing a waltz for many years. He also understood the Southern colonies used the French version of the waltz at their balls.

Stanton made sure his plans were in place, and then spent most of the day with the Durks. He had to make an effort not to start pacing the floor, and Reverend Durk laughed at his anxiousness.

At two o'clock, Stanton could stand it no longer, and he headed for the church. Ralph would help collect Mr. Evans. Since Stanton had no family or close friends, he'd chosen not to have a man stand up with him.

By two-thirty, the church had started to fill. As his grandmother had always said, people loved weddings and funerals because it gave them a chance to get together.

At a quarter to three, the men carried Mr. Evans inside and set his chair in front of the first bench. He looked alert and pleased. For the first time, Stanton saw him dressed in a suit, and he looked distinguished. He glanced over at Stanton and smiled.

Stanton took a deep breath. It wouldn't be long now.

The minister came to get him, and the two of them took their places at the front. By now the crowd packed the church, and many more were still outside.

He heard a hush fall over the crowd, and as they stood, he saw Beth standing at the door on Reverend Durk's arm. As they started down the aisle, she took his breath away. The dress she wore looked as pretty as any he'd ever seen, and on her it looked stunning. It flowed long enough to cover her feet, so she slowly glided along with no sign of a limp.

The way she clutched Reverend Durk's arm, he knew nervousness gripped her. They stopped beside her father's chair, and she bent and kissed his forehead before taking the last few steps to stand with Stanton.

He couldn't have recounted what the ceremony had been like. He had stood too mesmerized by the woman beside him. He did hear her father call out that he gave her to this man. Stanton said his vows and listened as Beth gave hers. The preacher declared them man and wife and introduced them to the congregation. His heart leaped with joy. At last, Beth had become his wife.

They went down the aisle together as Mr. and Mistress Klein. There were so many well wishes, Stanton couldn't begin to remember them all. He did see Cecil come through the line, though, and he stiffened.

"You broke my heart, dear girl," he said to Beth.

She laughed. "I don't think so. We both know such a thing is impossible."

"I hope you know you are a very lucky man, Mr. Klein. You may have just won the only jewel among a herd of swine."

"That's the first thing I've ever heard you say, Mr. Shippen, with which I agree. At least, I agree that I've won a jewel, and I'm a blessed man because of it." At least the man admitted Stanton had won Beth. Did that mean he would finally back off?

When they joined the revelers outside, everything appeared ready. People were enjoying the food, and the musicians were playing a lively tune.

"They're waiting for you two to lead off the dancing," Mrs. Durk said.

"I couldn't," Beth pleaded in a panic and looked at Stanton.

Stanton whispered to Mrs. Durk the tune he wanted her to have the musicians play. He began to lead Beth to the center of the dance area.

"Please don't, Stanton. You know I can't dance."

"Trust me, Beth. I'm having the musicians play a slow waltz. I'll take you in my arms, and all you have to do is let me lead you. We won't step much. Just sway with the music. Whatever you did to come down the aisle without a falter, do it now."

"I stood on tiptoe with the shorter leg."

"That should work here too. Trust me, sweetheart. I'll hold you up."

The music started, and he took her into his arms. She looked into his eyes and stiffened with fear. They started moving with the music by taking tiny steps and swaying in time. He held her loosely against his body with a firm grasp so she'd know he held her secure.

"You're doing great," he told her. "I'm the envy of every man here. You are so beautiful, inside and out. No words can express how happy I am to have you for my wife."

He felt her relax against him, and he pulled her closer. After all, there could be no scandal in him dancing with his wife. The dance would have gone on and on if he'd had his say, but it ended all too soon. He put his arm around her waist as he led her to the side, and the crowd started clapping and cheering.

"Here you go," Mistress Durk said, and handed them each some cider. "Can I get you something to eat?"

Beth declined, so he did also. They sipped their cider and watched the dancers in a reel.

"Would you like to join the dancing, Mr. Klein?" Fiona stood before him. He had been so focused on Beth, he hadn't seen her approach. "I know Beth won't mind, since she could never dance a fast one with intricate steps."

"I would mind, because I don't want to leave my wife's side. I'm sure Cecil Shippen would be happy to dance with you. You and he seem to have much in common."

She gave Stanton a strange look and walked away without saying another word. He took Beth's hand in his.

"Are you ready to leave?" he asked.

"Yes."

They handed off their glasses to Mrs. Durk and thanked her. Beth said a special good-bye to her father, and the couple walked to the carriage where the driver waited.

"Drive to my farm, but take your time," Stanton told him.

He helped Beth inside, and then crawled in beside her. He put his arm around her, and she leaned her head on his shoulder.

"Tired?" he asked.

"A little. More from anxiety and nervousness than anything else."

"You needn't have worried. Everything went great, and it turned out to be a beautiful wedding."

"Yes, it did. Thank you for that, Stanton. Your plans were excellent."

"My plans weren't the beauty of today. You were."

She lifted her head and gave him a surprised look. "You say that like you mean it."

"I do. Every word. It's amazing to me that you have no sense of how pretty you really are."

She gave him a warm smile, and then glanced out the window of the carriage. "I never did make it out to see your farm. We planned the wedding too quickly."

"I thought I would show you around, when we get there today. That's one of the reasons I wanted to leave early, so you could see it before it got dark."

"What's the other reasons?" She put her hand on his shoulder, and he pulled her even closer.

"I want to be alone with you. At last, I can have you all to myself."

He bent and kissed her with all the emotion he felt. She took so much of his attention, he didn't even realize when they pulled up to the house.

Chapter Nine: The Honeymoon

"Good wives and good plantations are made by good husbands."

—Poor Richard's Almanack

"What's the driver going to do?" Beth asked as Stanton helped her out.

"His sister lives at the next farm. He'll stay there tonight and come for us in the morning."

Stanton took her bag. "Come, we'll start your tour with the house."

The carriage pulled off, and Beth looked up. "Oh, Stanton, it's a gorgeous house."

Stanton tried to see the house as Beth saw it. The two-story house had been made with varying shades of brown stones and mortar. The wooden shutters framed the windows, and the wooden shingles on the roof had turned a dark brown that matched the darker stones.

"My grandparents started out with a tiny log house. Ralph, my indentured servant, uses it now. They built this one after my parents married."

Stanton set her bag down on the porch, scooped her up, and carried her over the threshold. She weighed even less than he thought she would.

She had looped her hands around his neck, and he felt reluctant to put her down, but he gave her a light kiss and set her feet on the floor.

"Welcome home, Mistress Klein," he told her.

He retrieved her bag from the porch and began showing her the house. The parlor took up one end of the downstairs and the kitchen the other. A good-sized larder lay just off the kitchen.

"It's so big," Beth said, "and so well stocked. I can't imagine having spices to cook with. I've been lucky to keep salt, pepper, and sugar."

Upstairs there were two large chambers, one on each side of the hall. Stanton set her bag in his room.

"I hope it's agreeable with you to share my room. You could have your own across the hall, but I want you beside me."

She nodded and moved to the window at the end of the hall. She stood with her back to him as she looked over the farm.

"I love it, Stanton. Just look at this view."

"It's lovely," he said.

She turned, caught him looking at her and not out the window, and blushed. He took her hand.

"Do you want to see the outside?"

"Of course I do."

He showed her the root cellar and garden plot first. "I'm afraid I haven't planted much this year. I did plant the root crops, like carrots and potatoes, but I didn't get out any cabbage or other vegetables in the spring because planting the field crops took too much of my time."

"There may be time to put in cabbage as a fall crop, since they like cooler weather," she said. "I know we can sow some turnips for fall. I can take care of those. I know many people don't, but I love vegetables. I'm sure you prefer your meat."

"I'll at least help you prepare the soil for the cabbage and turnips. I do prefer my meat, but you can convince me to give vegetables a chance too, for I know you to be an excellent cook. And maybe you can make some kraut from those fall cabbages. Do you know how to make it?"

"Yes, I do."

Beth showed interest in everything. She inspected the barn, and grew excited over the animals. She walked beside the fields and praised his methods.

"Everything looks so well-tended. I'm very impressed."

"Perhaps it's a good thing I never brought you out to see the farm before we were married. Otherwise, I might have thought you wanted it and not me."

"Well, you know that's not true. I married only you, and the farm is an added blessing."

"I'm glad you like it. I want you to be happy here."

"How could I not?"

Not everyone likes a farm better than a town. Molly didn't.

"Are you hungry?" Beth asked when they returned to the house. "Shall I fix us some supper?"

"I am hungry, but I don't want you to take the time to cook a regular meal."

"I saw chickens outside. Do you have eggs, milk, and maybe cheese?"

"Yes to all of those. I bought some cheese and butter a few days ago."

"I can fix an egg dish in a few minutes."

"I have some bread to go with it, and there's cider."

Stanton stoked the fire and then sat at the table and watched Beth move around the kitchen to prepare their meal. He told her where to find a few things, and she set a plate before him in about twenty minutes. He said grace, because he knew she expected it, and they began eating. He had never eaten many eggs, outside of a few in baked goods, but this tasted delicious.

"I wish we had some preserves," he said, "but I've used all I had over the winter."

"I made a large crock of strawberry preserves. The blackberries will be ripening soon, and the grapes will be ready in the fall. Do you have any around here?"

"There're plenty of blackberries, and I'm sure we can find some wild grapes in the woods. There're nuts back there too, and I also have apple trees."

"Good, I can dry some, make a little apple butter, as well as pies, for us to use right away, and I know you'll want to make some cider."

He watched her excitement over the little things, and he became excited too. She seemed so enthusiastic and happy. He hoped she would stay that way.

Oh, Lord, please be with us tonight, he prayed silently. *Lead and direct me to be the husband Beth needs. Don't let me do anything to frighten her or hurt her, and bless our union, I pray. Amen.*

It seemed natural to be praying again. He had been the one with the stronger faith when married to Molly, but he had felt far removed from God over the past year. Now it seemed almost as if God was smiling at Stanton once more. After all, the Lord had granted him a wife, and what a blessing Beth seemed to be!

"Are you ready to retire?" he asked.

He saw Beth tense, and she hesitated before nodding. He stood, took her in his arms, kissed her with all the gentleness he could, and stroked her hair. She needed reassuring now.

"You go on up, get ready, and get into bed. I'll be up shortly. I promise you it will be all right. I won't do anything you don't want me to do."

He handed her a candle, and she left. He waited about twenty minutes and then carried his own candle to join her.

She had blown her candle out, but he set his on the candle stand. He noticed she had on a pretty bed gown—what he could see of it. She had the sheet pulled up beneath her arms. He took off most of his clothing, and Beth surprised him by watching. He blew out the candle, took off his remaining clothing, and got in bed with her. She lay as stiff as a board.

"Come here, darling. Let me just hold you."

He put his arm under her neck and shoulders and pulled her closer. She snuggled into his shoulder, and he wrapped his arms around her.

"Now, that's better. You know, I'm amazed by how well we've gotten to know each other in such short time. You're my best friend and confidant."

"Thank you. I feel that way about you too. I can talk to you just like I do my father, and I tell him everything."

He kissed her cheek, and she turned her face toward him. He took that as an invitation to kiss her mouth. Within a short time, she began responding with passion, as she had in the past. From there, one thing led to another in a natural progression. The joy he felt with her almost overwhelmed him.

Stanton awoke first the next morning, but he lay still, giving Beth extra time to sleep. He turned his head and watched her. He couldn't believe the reality of last night. It had to be a dream, but he should have recognized the fire and passion in her from the way she returned his kisses.

She was so different from Molly in every way. Molly had endured his attention as a duty required of her as his wife. She had never complained, but she never seemed to enjoy it or be a participant.

Beth had not just been there, she'd been his partner, and she gave every indication that she had enjoyed the night too. He just hoped in the light of day she wouldn't regret her passionate behavior.

He couldn't believe how different this wedding night had been from the first one. If he had to have both women for his wives, it was good Molly had been the first one. He hadn't known what he'd been missing until Beth. He would never have been satisfied with Molly once he'd known Beth.

How funny Beth had worried that he would constantly compare her with Molly. He'd done much more of that than he'd thought he would, but every time, Beth came out on top. He recognized more and more how much God had blessed him with his new wife.

Beth opened her eyes and smiled at him. That smile made his heart miss a beat.

She moved closer, laid her head on his chest, and he put his arm around her.

"How do you feel?" he asked.

"Wonderful."

His heart skipped two beats. Could heaven be any better than this? He wanted to kiss her, but he feared where that might lead, and he didn't want to aggravate any tenderness she might have. Besides, he didn't know what time the driver would have the carriage here. Instead, he kissed her on the forehead.

"I'll go down, get the fire going, and heat some water in the kettle. You stay in bed, and I'll bring you some warm water, so you can wash up. Then, while I milk the cow and feed the animals, you can fix us some breakfast. More eggs, like last night, would be fine, or you can cook porridge, if you'd rather."

"Are you trying to spoil me?"

"Yes, but, from what I've seen so far, I don't think it's going to be an easy job."

Beth stretched, and then turned onto her side and curled into a ball. She couldn't believe how worried she'd been over last night, when she should have listened to Stanton all along. He'd just failed to inform her that his lovemaking would be even better than his kisses.

Of course, he hadn't told her he loved her, but he'd shown her, hadn't he? He'd told her how much she meant to him. She had started to tell him she loved him a dozen times yesterday, but she'd held back. She wanted to wait for him to say it first. Otherwise, she'd be forcing him to say it back to her.

He'd been so patient and tender with her last night, until she had quit thinking and started just responding to him. She already looked forward to tonight. Now that she knew what to expect, it should be even better.

Thank you, dear Lord, for such a wonderful husband. Please bless our marriage and grant that I may be the wife Stanton wants and needs.

As much as she wanted to see her father, Beth almost hated to see the carriage pull up. She hated to leave the farm, but she'd be back soon. Her father would love it here too.

"How about a kiss for the road, Mistress Klein?" Stanton asked as they pulled away.

"You might get something started we can't finish, Mr. Klein," she teased.

"Oh, I don't know about that. This is an enclosed carriage."

"Stanton!"

He just grinned. Then he turned serious.

"You make me so happy, Beth. I never knew it could be possible for a man to feel this much happiness."

"You've made me very happy too."

"Do I, now? You have no regrets?"

"Well, maybe one."

"What's that?" He looked worried.

"That I couldn't have met you earlier, so we'd have had even more time together."

His face broke into a wide grin. She did love his smile.

"I'll agree with that."

Was he implying he'd rather have her instead of his first wife? She wouldn't ask and scolded herself for the thought.

Ralph met them at the door. "Thank goodness you're here. Your father's not doing well, but he refuses to let me fetch the doctor."

Beth rushed into the house, sat on her father's bed, and took his hand in hers. Her father looked pale, and the dullness in his eyes told her how much pain he had.

"Papa, what's wrong?"

"I feel like I have a millstone sitting on my chest."

His voice sounded weak and, even worse, lifeless.

"Do you want me to get the doctor?" Stanton whispered as he placed his hands on her shoulders in support.

She nodded, not taking her eyes from her father. Ralph left on some errand at the same time as Stanton went to get the doctor, but she didn't give it much heed.

She sat for minutes, just holding her father's hand. He had closed his eyes, and his breath had become shallow. Tears formed in her eyes, but she didn't bother to wipe them.

"Beth." He looked into her face.

"Yes, Papa."

"Are you happy with Stanton?"

"Yes, Papa. He's very tender in his treatment of me, and his farm is lovely. I can't wait for you to see it too."

"Good. I thought he'd be the man for you. Be happy, my dear one."

This sounded way too much like a good-bye, and Beth panicked.

"Papa, you can't leave me now. I need you. Don't you dare leave me!"

"I've tried so hard . . ."—he paused to get his breath—"to be here for you. So tired."

"But you need to be here to see your first grandchild. Remember?"

His mouth tried to turn upward into a smile, but it didn't quite make it. Beth felt her tears hitting her lap, but she paid them no mind.

"See from above. See your mama too." He closed his eyes.

"I love you, Papa. You've been both father and mother to me. What would I do without you?"

"Love you too," came a weak whisper, but his eyes remained closed. "Be happy."

His breath had become so shallow, she thought he had left her. When she put her ear to his chest, however, he still breathed.

Stanton returned with the doctor. Beth had no idea how long he'd been gone, but it couldn't have been as long as it seemed.

She stood to give the doctor access to the bed, and Stanton gathered her in his arms. She laid her head against him, and tried to borrow some of his strength.

"Here, darling. Sit down and try not to worry."

Stanton helped her to a chair and stood behind her with his hands on her shoulders. She needed both the chair and his touch. She felt as weak as a newborn colt.

The doctor took his time in examining the patient. His expression didn't look encouraging. At last, he cleared his throat.

"He's taken a decided turn for the worst, but I guess you knew that. Something has caused an unbalance, and the best treatment is bloodletting. I can do that now, with your permission."

"Are you sure that's best? He looks so pale."

"It will get rid of the impurities. You do want your father to get better, don't you?"

"Of course she does." Stanton spoke for her, and his voice had an edge to it.

"Very well then."

The doctor began to gather the items from his bag he would need. Beth moved over to the kitchen and began preparing her father a little porridge for breakfast. She couldn't bear to watch the doctor take the blood, and she took care not to look that way.

Stanton followed her and sat down on the back bench at the table. She saw concern etched on his face, and it made her feel better. She wouldn't be alone in this.

"What can I do to help?" he asked.

"Just your being here helps." She took his hand, and he squeezed her fingers. "We need to pray. That's all I know to do."

He nodded and lowered his head. She did the same and said her own silent prayer.

When she looked up at Stanton, he gave her a weak smile. She felt his desire to make everything better and his realization that he couldn't. At this point, no one could.

"For where two or three are gathered in my name, there am I in the midst of them," he said, and Beth recognized the verse from Matthew.

"You know your Bible well," she said, impressed with his memory.

"I memorized some verses when I attended school," he told her.

Chapter Ten: The Funeral

"At night lay down prepar'd to have thy sleep, thy death, thy bed, thy grave."

—The New England Primer

"How much do I owe you, Doctor?" Beth asked the man when he'd finished.

"Never mind," the physician said. "It's all been taken care of."

Beth showed the man out, and then turned to Stanton. She didn't even have to ask the question. He knew what she wanted.

"You and your father are my family now, Beth. It's my responsibility to take care of you."

Somehow, the words didn't sit well with her, but she said nothing. She knew he wanted to do what he could to help, but, for the first time, she felt as if she'd lost some of her independence. She tried to tell herself it would be nice to have someone take care of her and not to have to worry about funds, but the thought did little to dispel the troubling sense of something she didn't quite understand herself.

"I sent Ralph home in the wagon and told him to come back tomorrow afternoon."

"You should have gone with him, Stanton. There's little you can do here, but you're needed there."

She could tell by the look on his face her words had hurt him, although she hadn't intended for them to. She didn't mean for it to sound as if she didn't need him.

"There's no place for you to sleep," she added, knowing it sounded lame as soon as it left her mouth.

"I doubt you'll be sleeping much, so I can sit up with you. I couldn't leave you alone with your father's health deteriorating like it is. I'd get no sleep at the farm for worrying about you. I've gotten little sleep over the last year, anyway—except for last night, that is. I'll be fine."

Beth understood, then, that Stanton needed her as much as she needed him—maybe more so. She also saw how insecure he seemed at that moment. She'd always seen him as rock solid and self-confident. He seemed to fear Papa might die with her alone with him, and that possibility scared her too.

"I'm glad you're here," she told him with sincerity. "I'm glad you're with me."

He sighed and put his arms around her. She felt his strength envelope her.

"Always, darling. I'll always be here for you."

They sat side by side in chairs pulled close enough together to hold hands. Her father didn't stir. Beth got up several times to spoon water into his mouth and check on him. He would swallow a little water, but he didn't respond otherwise.

"Can we make a pallet on the floor here?" Stanton asked later in the night. "You'd be more comfortable if you could stretch out."

"We both would," she said. "I sleep on one in the loft because the space is too low for a bed. You could help me move it down here."

Even with all the commotion of getting the mattress and bedding moved down, Beth's father didn't move or wake.

Beth lay down on her side and faced her father. Stanton did the same behind her, and pulled her close to him. They fit together like stacked spoons.

"Take a nap, Beth. If your father wakes, we'll hear him."

Beth didn't think she could possibly have slept, but she must have. When she awoke, the room had lightened. She moved to stand, and Stanton sat up too.

"I'll stoke the fire and put on some water for tea," he told her.

She went to her father and noted his skin had grown even whiter. She touched his hand, and it felt cool and unresponsive. A sound must have come from her lips because Stanton came to her side in an instant. He took one look at the situation and pulled her into his arms.

"He didn't suffer," he whispered into her hair. "He went in his sleep, like most of us would choose to go, if we could."

With that, reality hit her hard, and she screamed for her father. Tears began to roll, and sobs shook her entire body. Stanton stood with her, holding her and stroking her hair, as one would caress a favorite pet. Beth didn't know how long they stayed like that, but when she pulled back, she saw she had soaked Stanton's shirt with her tears.

"Give me some time to collect myself," she told Stanton.

She hoped he didn't see her need to be alone as rejecting his presence, but she needed time to herself, as much as a man making a long journey across the desert needed water. She went out back and sat on the bench placed against the house.

Stanton had been right. Her father had died peacefully in his sleep. He would never suffer again. He'd be walking the streets of gold with her mother by his side. She shouldn't be wishing him back, but she did.

Her father had been her everything since her mother had died. He'd buried his wife, sucked in his grief, and taken care of his daughter, while he let her believe she was the one taking care of him.

Though the years, he'd taught her things she needed to know—household things, as well as how to farm. He'd even taken on her mother's role to teach her facts a girl needed to know. After his accident and their move to the village, he'd taken over her education, and he'd taught her well. As a result, she had a better education than most men. Although her father had pushed her to be her best, he also encouraged her and believed in her. She would miss him dearly.

She gathered up her courage and went back inside. She saw Stanton had rolled up their pallet and put it back in the loft. He now sat in a chair, with his elbows propped on his legs and his head in his hands. He didn't hear her come up, but she stopped behind him and wrapped her arms around his shoulders. He instantly sat straighter and patted her hands.

"Are you all right?" he asked.

She kissed the top of his head. "I'm all right. Will you help me prepare his body?"

She would have preferred to do the task alone as her last act of love for her father, but she sensed Stanton wanted to do something to help. For some reason, he needed to be included, as if he required proof of her commitment to him.

As it turned out, his help made the job much easier. He didn't talk much as they took care of the preparations, and the silence helped Beth. She could work through her own thoughts.

After they had the body washed and dressed, Beth's minister came by. He'd heard of her father's turn for the worst from the doctor and had come to check on him and offer prayers. Stanton left to order the coffin, while Beth talked with her pastor.

The doctor came next, and then began a procession of women who came to help and offer condolences. When the coffin arrived, the men helped move the body and set it up for viewing.

Stanton acted as host for the men who came. Many of them came in but soon left to stand outside and talk. The cottage was too small to make large groups comfortable.

Agatha Denny took over inside, and Beth let her organize everything because the day had become a blur to her. Beth went through the motions and said the right things, but she felt numb and lifeless.

There would be people in the house all night, but Mistress Denny insisted Beth go up to the loft and rest if she couldn't sleep. Beth soon learned one did not say no to Mistress Denny once the woman made up her mind about something.

Even as exhausted as she'd become, Beth couldn't even doze. The rafters creaked and groaned, as if they too had trouble settling for the night. When Stanton eased up the ladder and lay down beside her, she snuggled into him and fell asleep, like a candle being snuffed out for the night.

When she awoke the next morning, Stanton had already gone down, but she couldn't find him downstairs. She asked the first person she saw where he had gone.

"He rented a horse and went to your farm to see about some things but said to tell you he'd be back as soon as he could."

Beth felt a void. She recognized then how much she needed Stanton. For one thing, without him she would be all alone and forced to marry someone much less suitable. A single woman who'd never been married would not be allowed to live alone. Unless a family might be willing to take her in, she would be forced to wed. But her need for Stanton went far beyond that. In a short time, he had become a vital part of her.

Stanton came back about noon. Beth hadn't eaten anything earlier, so she sat and ate a few bites with him from the food the women had prepared.

"Could we walk down to the creek?" she asked.

She needed some time alone with him, and the idea seemed to please him. He took her hand as they started out.

"I hated to leave this morning without telling you good-bye, but I decided the earlier I left, the earlier I could return, and I wanted you to get as much rest as possible." His eyes pleaded with her to understand.

"When I woke up and found you'd gone, I realized how much I missed you and how much I need you." She reached out and put her hand on his arm.

"Then, something good came from it. I missed you too, you know. I found it hard to be in the house without you. I checked on the farm, but I also brought back my clothes for tomorrow."

"Some of the women took the beige lace off my dark-green dress and added some black trim, so I'll wear that. There won't be time to make a black one right away."

"I doubt if your father would have wanted you in black. Is there anything else I can do to help you? Do you need anything?"

"Just being here with me helps. Thank you for all you've done." Beth took a deep breath. Except for Stanton, her world had been shattered. She couldn't believe she'd never see her father again this side of heaven. Tears silently washed her face.

"I wish I could do more. I wish I could take away all your grief and hurt. I hate this even happened." He reached for her hand, and she appreciated the extra strength it gave her.

"I think Father struggled to be here for me." She swallowed back the tears. "I think he knew he didn't have long, but he managed to see me settled through sheer will. He pushed me to marry you sooner rather than later. I understand now, and I respect him for it."

"You're not sorry we didn't have a longer courtship or feel pressured to do something you didn't want to?"

"I'm not sorry at all. There's much to be said for discovering more about each other as husband and wife. I didn't feel pressured either. My father would have never forced me to marry someone against my will."

"I'd agree there's much joy in getting to know each other as husband and wife." He gave her a hint of a smile.

He took her in his arms and kissed her gently, as if she were delicate and might break if he squeezed. Her heart felt heavy with love for him. Afterward, they sat beside the creek.

"My grandparents, parents, Molly, and the baby are buried at the farm. Would you like to bury your father there? It would be closer to us than if you buried him in the village, and I'd like for us to be buried there someday too."

She paused to consider his offer. She hadn't really thought about where her father would be buried. She'd been too occupied with getting through each moment. "How would the graves be arranged?"

"You can choose the plot for your father and us. All I ask is that you and I be side by side."

"Okay. I'd like for Father's grave to be near, where I could tend it."

"Then, we can have the funeral tomorrow, load the coffin on the wagon, and bury him at the farm. We can come back on Saturday and move your things."

She tried to hold back the tears again, but they broke through with a sob. Stanton reached out and pulled her to him. He held her and let her cry against him, and his arms gave her comfort, more comfort than she would have imagined.

Six men carried the coffin from the cottage to the church on Friday. Beth and Stanton walked behind the coffin. Next, came friends and neighbors in double file. The pastor did a good job with the eulogy and service.

By clutching Stanton's hand or having his arm around her, Beth managed to get through the funeral and shed only silent tears. She dreaded the burial more.

The bearers loaded the coffin in the wagon, Stanton helped Beth into the seat, and he drove to the farm. The pastor and a small group of mourners followed.

The whole affair became much harder for Beth when she had to watch the coffin be put into the ground. She tried to tell herself her father wasn't in that box. His spirit had already gone to heaven, but, seeing the coffin lowered and dirt thrown on top it made everything seem so final. She would never again see her father in this lifetime.

The dam burst, and she couldn't control the sobs. Stanton grabbed her with gentle hands and guided her back to the house. The service had ended anyway.

Stanton put her in their bedroom while he went down to see to the guests. He must've realized she didn't want to talk to anyone now. He had been so understanding. Had he felt this way when Molly had died? Like her, Stanton had lost all of his immediate family. They had only each other now.

She lay for a while, but she found herself too jittery, so she got up and looked around the room. She hadn't had a chance to explore any of the house on her own.

She saw Stanton's things, and her wedding dress. A trunk held bed linens, but nothing of Molly's things remained. Beth had hoped to find a portrait, miniature, or drawing of her, but she didn't.

She'd tried to stifle her curiosity about Stanton's first wife, but it hadn't worked. She wondered, not just how Molly had looked, but how she'd acted and how they'd gotten along. She tried not to be jealous of a dead woman, but it bothered her to think of Molly lying in Stanton's arms, sharing his kisses, and being intimate with him.

Maybe she shouldn't have married a widower, but she felt certain she was meant to be Stanton's wife. She couldn't imagine what her life would be like now without him. She'd have to learn to push thoughts of Molly away, and do her best to live with Stanton in the present. She just hoped he would do the same. The fear he might be wishing he had Molly back cut her even deeper than her father's death.

When everyone had left, Stanton came upstairs to find her sitting up. "I thought you'd be resting."

"I couldn't settle down."

"Come down and eat some supper with me. Our friends brought more food. I put some of it in the springhouse."

"I'm not very hungry."

"Then, at least come down and get some tea and sit with me while I eat."

The food did look good, and she let Stanton coax her into fixing a small plate. Before Stanton said grace, he took her hand in his. Beth liked how it felt to pray joined like that.

When she started eating, she realized how hungry she'd become. Stanton looked pleased when she ate most of the food on her plate.

Do you want to stay up awhile or go to bed now? We could play some chess."

"You know you could beat me now. Are you trying to take unfair advantage of me?"

She'd meant to tease, but Stanton's grimace indicated he thought she'd been serious. She knew he wanted to distract her from the grief. Since her father's death, she'd been hurting him, when she didn't mean to. This hadn't happened when they were courting. Why now?

"I think I'd rather go to bed, if you're ready." Beth said.

"I could sleep in the other room for tonight, if you'd rather."

"No, I prefer you to sleep with me, like we did after our wedding."

Stanton looked at his wife and tried to decipher what she'd meant. Did she want the same attention he'd given her on their wedding night? His pulse did a lively dance at the thought. But, no, she must be tired and want him to mold around her like he had last night. He'd felt certain she'd be awake the entire time, but she fell asleep as soon as he lay down beside her, and that had made him feel good.

"Come then."

He took her hand and led her upstairs. Last time he'd given her time to undress, but this time he wanted to watch her.

At first she seemed surprised, but she laid out her bed gown and began to undress layer after layer at an unhurried pace. When she removed the last one, she rushed to slide into her gown, but not before he saw her beauty. Even the thin material of the gown revealed a perfect figure.

He knew it would unnerve her if he stood there and stared, so he undressed too, but he managed to watch Beth all the same. He blew out the candle and slipped in beside her.

She hurried over to lay her head on his shoulder. He rejoiced to have her here with him and wanting to be in his arms. He still had trouble believing she wanted him too.

She reached over and put her lips on his and began a kiss. He thought about remaining still to see what she would do, but he couldn't. His lips responded to hers in the same way his lungs breathed in air or his heart pumped blood.

She wiggled even closer, and he had no doubt about what she wanted. He wanted it too. For whatever reason, she needed him tonight, and for a multitude of reasons, he would always need her.

Chapter Eleven: Cecil

"Suspicion may be no Fault, but shewing it may be a great one."

—Poor Richard's Almanack

"Beth, how much shorter is your one leg?" Stanton asked at breakfast the next morning.

"About an inch, I guess. Why do you ask?"

"Just curious."

"Does it bother you?"

"Only in that it's made things more difficult for you. I admire that you haven't let it stop you."

"It does slow me down some, though." She laughed. He liked her ability to laugh at herself. She hadn't let bitterness take root. Her grief over the loss of her father seemed to have eased a bit, too, at least for moments.

"How much from the cottage do you want to move here? Do I need to bring Ralph along to help?"

"None of the furniture, unless you want to set up another bed in the other upstairs chamber here. There's my spinning wheel, however. Otherwise, it's just my clothes, my mother's trunk, an armload of books, the chess set, my sewing basket, and a little from the kitchen. Are we going to keep the cottage? Father bought it after we sold our farm."

"It might be better to rent it for now, if that's agreeable to you." Stanton didn't think she'd be ready to let go of the cottage yet, and he didn't mind keeping it.

"It is."

"Good. I'll let the two ministers know, as well as Mr. Mueller at the store."

"Tell Mistress Denny too. She likes to be the bearer of news, and she'll let everyone know it's available."

"Good idea."

It didn't take long to load the wagon and set the cottage to order. Beth had packed them some dinner, but they were finished before dinnertime.

"I have some business to take care of," Stanton told her. "I'll drop you off at the Muellers' store. Get anything you want and charge it to my account. I'm not planning to come back anytime soon, except for Sundays. We can stop and eat our food on the way home."

Stanton took care of his business and hurried back to the store. He walked in to find Cecil talking to Beth in a back corner. The rogue had his hand on her upper arm, as he tried to convince her of something. Stanton wanted to rush over and knock the arm away. How dare Cecil touch his wife!

"How do I even know it's my child?" Cecil asked as Stanton got closer.

Stanton froze. He couldn't have moved for any reason. All his blood seemed to drain from his head. For the first time in his life, he feared he might lose consciousness.

Neither had noticed him yet, but Beth looked up first. She took a step back from Cecil, and the cad dropped his hand and looked around.

"I'll talk to you later, Beth," Cecil said. He nodded in acknowledgment of Stanton, and made a hasty retreat well out of Stanton's reach.

Stanton's blood began to boil. Had he been wrong about Beth? Had she married him, while she carried another man's child? He couldn't believe that of her, and on their wedding night he'd been certain she'd never been with a man before. He took a deep breath and tried to push his anger down, but it didn't want to retreat.

"Are you ready?" he asked her. He tried to keep the disgust from his voice, but instead it came out cold and without feeling.

He did offer her his arm, and her hand trembled as she took it. Good. She needed to be uncertain. He sure felt that way.

He pushed her into the wagon seat, and they started off. Neither said anything at first, and a wall began to rise between them.

Beth broke their silence first. "I'm sorry, but Cecil came to talk to me. He's always talked to me when he's needed advice or help because he says I'm the only one he trusts to listen without judging him."

"How would you feel if you found me talking to the Widow Knotts, and she had her hand on my arm? What if we were talking about a baby?" His voice came out harsh and angry.

"I know it looked bad, but it was quite innocent."

"You didn't answer my question, Beth. How would you feel?"

"I wouldn't like it, but I hope I would listen to your side of things before I jumped to any conclusions."

"All right, I'm listening. I heard Cecil say the baby might not be his, so explain."

Beth sucked in her breath. That couldn't be a good sign. He looked at her face. She looked concerned, but not ashen or guilty. If she carried someone else's child, could he treat it as his own? What irony that would be, when he'd sought a wife to gain an heir.

"Cecil was talking about Fiona. She told him he's gotten her with child, and she expects him to marry her."

Most of Stanton's anger left with the same speed it had come. He didn't like that Cecil had used Beth as his confidant, but she hadn't been involved with Cecil on a deeper level. At least, she wasn't having his child. He believed her because what she said made sense with what he already knew. Hadn't he seen Fiona sneak out to meet someone alone? He'd thought at the time it might be Cecil.

He also wondered if this was why Fiona became available to him right after he started courting Beth. Had she been afraid Cecil wouldn't marry her, and she decided to secure a husband another way? The thought sent chills through his body, despite the warm day.

"Please forgive me for acting like a fool. I'm sorry I got so upset when I saw you with Cecil. I've never liked him, and what you said now confirms how I feel. I'd prefer you stay away from him."

"To be honest, I'd like to, but without being rude and unchristian, I don't see how. He's been living only for himself, and he needs someone to get him on the right road."

"Beth, that's not your job."

"Whose job is it then? If you'll take over, I'd be pleased, but you admitted you don't like Cecil, so you don't seem to be the best one to lend a hand. I believe God uses His people to help others. Isn't that what the Bible teaches?"

"But you're my wife, not Cecil Shippen's."

"And I'm very thankful for that, but did marrying you mean I'm to lock myself away from the world? Does it mean I should desert those who need me?"

"In this case, it does. You're being too naive and innocent where Cecil is concerned. I need you, Beth. I don't want you befriending someone like Cecil Shippen. By your own words, he's a reprobate, and I don't trust the man. I'm not being unreasonable. As your husband, it's my job to protect you and keep you safe. Promise me you won't see him again."

"I didn't plan to talk with him today, but he came up to me in the store, and we were in a public place. Can't we compromise on this, Stanton? I'll promise I'll never meet him in private, and I'd never allow him to flirt with me. I'll also agree to tell you every time we talk. Won't this be good enough?"

Stanton sighed. What Beth said sounded very reasonable, but he still didn't like it. "I'll consider what you've said. I do trust you, but I don't trust Cecil."

He reached for her hand and kissed it. She slipped closer to him in the wagon seat and smiled.

They stopped the wagon beside a meadow, took a blanket from the back, and spread it out under a shade tree. They sat and ate their dinner as birds serenaded. When they'd finished, Stanton moved to lean back against the tree trunk and motioned for Beth to sit beside him.

"Do you think I'm being unreasonable or overbearing as far as Cecil is concerned?" he asked as he pulled her against him.

"No, I understand your feelings stem from your caring. If I were in your place, I might feel the same, but if you were in my place, I think you'd feel the same as I do."

"We'll try your compromise and see how it works. Just don't keep secrets from me."

"I don't plan to." She almost snapped her answer. "I would've told you about talking with Cecil today."

Stanton didn't like where this conversation seemed to be headed, but he couldn't drop it now. "Including the part about Fiona's dilemma?"

"Yes, including that. When Cecil asked me to keep the secret, I told him I kept no secrets from my husband." She sounded calmer.

He hugged her tighter and kissed the top of her head. That led to a real kiss, which left him wanting more.

"Come," he said, getting up. "Let's go home."

Stanton spent the rest of Saturday with Beth, but he knew the idyllic days were drawing to an end. After tomorrow, he would have to begin the farm work in earnest again. He'd already allotted too much time away for courting, and autumn would soon be upon them. Harvest season made a farmer's life busy indeed.

Ralph had always eaten breakfast and dinner in the main house and taken his supper to his cabin. Stanton decided he wanted to have Beth all to himself at breakfast too, so he told Beth to keep Ralph supplied with bread, butter, and preserves, or something he could eat for breakfast on his own. She could fix enough for dinner for them all, and send something with Ralph for his supper. This would all start Monday.

Sunday, Stanton and Beth slept later than usual, and when they awoke, they lay in each other's arms and talked. Then they realized how late it had become, ate a quick breakfast, and began getting ready for church.

"We'll go to the Presbyterian church today," Stanton told her, "but I'd like to visit with the Durks afterward. I need to explain to the reverend why I've decided to start attending your church."

"Oh, and why is that?"

Stanton grinned. "Mainly because I get to sit beside my beautiful wife."

"Now, that's a good reason to choose a church," Beth teased.

"I think so." His grin widened.

The service went well, but the gossip afterward implied that Fiona had gone to Boston for an extended visit with an aunt. Stanton and Beth looked at the other, and Beth also seemed aware that Cecil must have refused to marry Fiona.

Stanton hoped Cecil wouldn't become even more of a pest with Fiona gone. He couldn't understand why Cecil didn't want to marry the woman. They seemed to like each other well enough. Despite their compromise, he hoped Cecil stayed away from Beth. He couldn't tolerate the thought of them being together, even in public.

Some of the younger girls who'd associated with Fiona called Beth over to talk with them. The cobbler came up and gave Stanton a wrapped package, which he took to the wagon and hid under the tarp. When he came back to the churchyard, he found Beth looking for him.

Cecil stood talking with some of the men, but his eyes found Beth as often as he dared. Stanton stiffened. The situation seemed to be getting worse, and he didn't know how much longer he could stand it. He glared at Cecil, and the rogue looked away.

"Where were you?" Beth asked.

"I went to the wagon. Are you ready to go?"

They drove to the Durks. As Stanton expected, they were invited to dinner. Stanton relaxed when Beth began helping Mistress Durk, as if they were old friends. After dinner, Beth helped clean up, and Stanton and Reverend Durk went into the parlor to talk. Stanton explained that he and Beth would be attending the Presbyterian church.

"Why have you decided to go there?" Reverend Durk asked.

"We were torn as to where we wanted to go, but to be honest, I enjoy sitting beside Beth during the service. We'll miss you and Mistress Durk, however."

"There's been talk of not separating the men and women in our Lutheran churches. I believe it will happen, but it might not be soon. Just because you're attending another church doesn't mean you aren't welcome here. We consider you our friends, so please come by anytime you can."

"Thank you. I appreciate that."

When they arrived back at the farm, Stanton got the package from the wagon. He just hoped his idea would work.

"What is that?" Beth asked.

"Come inside, and I'll show you."

He had her sit down and handed her the package to unwrap. Out came a pair of new shoes.

"How did you know I needed new shoes?"

"These aren't just any shoes. Try them on."

As she started to do so, she noticed the difference. Her head jerked up, and her face filled with questions.

"Just try them on and see if they work. I'm hoping they will make it easier on you."

She put the shoes on, and walked across the room. Stanton felt certain no one would notice her barely discernible limp now.

"These are fantastic! Wherever did you find them?'

"I had the cobbler make them. He built up the sole and heel on the one shoe about an inch. That shoe is going to be stiffer, but there shouldn't be a discrepancy in the height, so it should be easier for you to walk."

"This is much better, and when I get used to them, it should be even easier. I've often had backaches, and the doctor thought they might come from the way I have to walk. These should help with those too. Thank you! Thank you so much. They're wonderful. You're wonderful!" She rushed over and hugged him.

Stanton felt pleased. He wrapped his arms around her and relished the feel of her. He had to keep reminding himself she was his. It still seemed unreal much of the time.

"Since we'll be eating something simple for supper tonight, and you won't need to cook," he told her, "why don't we rest for a while? I think I could use an afternoon nap. What about you, Mistress Klein?"

Chapter Twelve: Ralph

"The discontented man finds no easy chair."

—Poor Richard's Almanack

Monday, Stanton ate breakfast and took Ralph to the fields. They had much to do, because Ralph hadn't accomplished as much as he should have while Stanton had been courting and getting married.

When they came back for dinner, Beth had the garden prepared for planting cabbage and turnips. She also had dinner ready.

"You should have told me, and I'd have helped you prepare the soil," Stanton told her.

"I knew you had enough to do, and I enjoyed working in a garden again."

"Well, in the spring, when you'll be planting more, I'll use the oxen to plow it up."

Stanton noticed Ralph's surprised look when he tasted Beth's cooking. She had outdone herself.

"I believe this is the best meal I've ever had," the servant told her.

"Thank you," she replied without turning around to look at him.

The problem grew. Stanton was glad Ralph didn't eat more than one meal a day at the house, and that seemed to be one too many. The man watched Beth's every move. He tried to do it so no one noticed, and Beth didn't appear to, but Stanton did, and it made him angry. He'd never experienced feelings of jealousy before, and he didn't like them, but he found he couldn't stop them.

Ralph also tried to work around the house as much as possible. He brought in firewood without being asked, wanted to haul up water from the spring for washday, and often asked Beth if she needed his help with anything.

Stanton didn't know what to do about it. Should he tell the man to quit being so nice to his wife and stop trying to help her? He even questioned if he might be too sensitive and jealous, but he didn't think so. He knew what he'd seen with his own eyes.

In the end, he tried to keep Ralph working away from the house as much as possible, and Stanton tried to take care of the things nearer. He even took over all the milking so Ralph wouldn't be carrying the milk into the house to give to Beth.

Stanton liked this arrangement better. He liked being around Beth too, and a part of him could understand how Ralph felt. But Stanton was her husband and not Ralph or Cecil. Neither man should look at her with interest. Why did these men have problems treating her as Mistress Klein?

The days fell into a routine. Stanton and Ralph did outside chores, most of which involved the fields. Beth tended her fall garden, gathered eggs, cooked, kept house, did the laundry, and took care of countless other tasks, especially those that would get them ready for winter.

Her built-up shoe made it so much easier for her that Stanton had one of her old shoes fixed the same way so she could use them for the dirtier jobs, like gardening.

Stanton and Ralph came in from the fields late one afternoon to find Beth moving a dead snake with her hoe. The snake had been decapitated.

"What happened?" Stanton asked.

"I came upon a snake as I worked in the garden. It came crawling out of the section where I'm not planning to plant anything now."

"Did you kill it?" Ralph asked.

What a foolish question! Stanton thought.

"I did."

"Beth," Stanton said, "this is a poisonous one."

"I know. It's a copperhead. That's why I killed it. I would have left it to eat mice if it had been nonpoisonous, like a garter snake or a black racer."

"You should have called me. I don't want you dealing with poisonous snakes."

"By the time I found you, the snake would have been gone, and I'd forever be wondering where it might turn up. It seemed better to kill it when I had the hoe in my hand."

"Weren't you scared?" Ralph asked. His tone of concern irked Stanton. The man seemed way too solicitous to Stanton's wife.

"Not really, although I took care. At least, I managed to see it in plenty of time. It would have been worse to run upon it unaware."

"I still don't like it," Stanton said. "I'm going to have the foundry make us a bell we can mount beside the house, so you can call me from the fields if you need me."

"I appreciate your concern, Stanton, but I can take care of a snake."

"I agree with Mr. Klein," Ralph said. "You shouldn't be dealing with a dangerous copperhead."

Beth ignored the servant this time. She turned to Stanton.

"If you'd feel better to have a bell, then that's fine, but if I can handle the situation without calling you, I will. As you can see, I dealt with this."

She flung the dead copperhead from the end of her hoe to an area of weeds away from the house. Stanton took the hoe from her and handed it to Ralph to put in the toolshed.

"Come, darling. Let's go inside."

He put his arm around her waist and led her toward the house. He felt Ralph's eyes on them the whole way. When they started in the door, he looked back, and Ralph had just begun to turn away.

He thought perhaps he should give Ralph more time off, so he could find his own woman. The servant's bond wouldn't be up for two more years, and he couldn't marry until then, but perhaps an evening in the village would help. He made a mental note to give him the afternoon off once a month on a regular basis.

"How much more time does Ralph have on his indenture?" Beth asked when they were in the kitchen. Could she read his mind?

"About two years. Why do you ask?" Was Beth interested in the man?

"I just wondered. How old is he?"

"He was twenty-one when I bought his indenture, so that would make him around twenty-six now. Why this sudden interest in Ralph?"

"I don't know. In some way, I feel uncomfortable around him, but I'm not sure why. He hasn't done or said anything to make me feel that way. I may just be too sensitive."

Stanton caught himself before he let out a sigh of relief. He needed to gain control of his jealousy. The emotion came as such a new one for him. He had no experience with how to deal with it, but Ralph had never looked at Molly the way he did Beth.

Early the next morning, Stanton made his way to the kitchen to rekindle the fire. In the dim light, he could barely see. He hurried to take care of the fire and made his way to the barn.

He had just brought in the cow and started milking, when an ear-splitting scream shattered the quiet. Stanton sprang to his feet and raced across the yard to the house. He'd never heard Beth scream, not even over finding the copperhead. *Something must be terribly wrong.*

He flung open the door, and a hysterical Beth rushed into his arms. She buried her face into his chest, and he felt her body trembling.

"What is it, sweetheart?" he asked.

She appeared too distraught to answer. Stanton looked over her head to see what could have caused this. At first he could see nothing out of the ordinary, but then he noticed two severed chicken heads lying on the table with the bloody parts at the table's edge. In his place lay the head of a rooster and in Beth's a hen's. His arms tightened around her, as if by sheer force he could take the grotesque images away.

"Shhh. It's okay, darling. It's nothing that will hurt you."

She took a deep breath, trying to pull herself together, when Ralph came busting in. He stopped and stared at Beth.

"What have you done to her?" he demanded of Stanton with his fists clenched at his sides.

"Watch what you're saying, Ralph. Beth's been frightened. Look on the table. Do you know anything about that?"

Ralph paled when he saw the chicken heads. Was it guilt or a reaction to the bizarre table setting?

"Are you accusing me of putting those ghastly heads on the table? I would never do anything to frighten the lady."

Stanton pondered the truth in Ralph's words. Perhaps he hoped Beth would suspect Stanton, but that seemed a bit farfetched.

"Would you clean those up while I take Mistress Klein upstairs?"

Stanton led Beth away before Ralph had a chance to say anything else. The nerve of the man insinuating Stanton had done something to upset Beth!

Once he had her in the bedroom, she calmed down. He sat her on the bed and brought her a damp cloth for her eyes.

"I'm sorry. I made such a scene," she said. "It was just so unexpected and such a shock."

"I understand. I don't blame you for being distressed." He threw the cloth in the basin and took her in his arms. "I can't imagine who would do such a thing, but the fact that someone had to have come into the house and maliciously put them there makes it so much worse."

Beth took a deep breath. "Come, I'll fix your breakfast." Stanton looked at her in amazement. He could tell she wanted to quit talking about the incident, though.

"No, I told Ralph to clean up the mess, but you stay here and rest for a while. I'll put some of those wonderful strawberry preserves you made on a piece of bread, and that will be enough for my breakfast."

"No, I'd rather be busy. If I lie here, the images will be too vivid. I'll come down and get breakfast."

"I'll just have a look around to make sure the house is safe now, and then I'll finish milking. Are you sure you're all right?"

"Of course, and thank you."

"For what?"

"For running to me without pause, for being my support and comforter, and for not making me feel foolish."

"I'm your husband, Beth, and I'll always be those things for you and more. You're important to me."

He and Beth ate breakfast together, but they didn't sit where the severed chicken heads had been placed, even though Ralph had done a good job of cleaning them up. As he ate, Stanton tried to figure out who had done the deed. The most logical choices he could come up with were Ralph or Cecil, but he couldn't imagine what their motives could be. Cecil seemed the better choice, because he had told Beth she would regret rejecting him. Yes, Cecil must have been out to scare Beth for revenge. He gritted his teeth. The man would do well to leave the Kleins alone, if he knew what was good for him.

Stanton felt reluctant to leave her at the house by herself, but she did seem to have recovered, and she assured him she would be fine. He still had much to do, so he dragged himself to the fields.

The rest of the day progressed without any more problems, but Stanton replayed the incident in his mind. A chill ran through him that someone had come into their home like that with them asleep upstairs; someone had invaded their privacy. They could have been murdered in their beds. He couldn't get either possible culprit out of his head. Could Ralph be trying to make Beth think Stanton had tried to unnerve her, or was Cecil to blame? It would likely be someone who knew Beth.

That evening, Stanton double-checked all the doors and windows on the house, trying to figure out how the intruder got in. He saw nothing out of the ordinary.

Stanton let Ralph have Saturday afternoon off, and Ralph borrowed a horse and rode into town. Stanton didn't know how late he stayed away, but he had returned and hitched up the wagon for them to take to church Sunday morning.

Stanton told the sheriff about the chicken heads left in their kitchen when he saw the man at church.

"It sounds like someone's idea of a prank to me," the sheriff said, "but let me know if you have any more trouble. In the meantime, I'll keep my eyes and ears open."

When Stanton and Beth got back home, he couldn't find Ralph. He didn't come when Stanton called him to unhitch the wagon, and his cabin stood empty, although all his things seemed to be there. Had he run away?

Ralph didn't appear Monday morning either. If he'd run away, he would be committing a crime by breaking his bond, but Stanton figured he'd have taken his things, if that were the case.

Stanton didn't see a sign of him Tuesday. He went to Middleville to inform the sheriff that Ralph had gone missing. He took Beth along because, after the chicken head incident, he didn't feel comfortable leaving her at the farm alone.

Beth stayed in the wagon while he went in to talk with the sheriff. He had just started out the door, when he ran into Horace Sneed, Molly's brother. Stanton hadn't seen him since Molly's funeral, and Stanton had forgotten how much the man looked like Molly.

Horace was shorter and stockier than Stanton, but he presented himself well. In fact, the features that he shared with his sister looked better on the man than they had the woman. Yet, the medium brown hair and light brown eyes seemed common enough.

"Horace, it's good to see you. What are you doing in Middleville? Have you moved from Philadelphia?"

"No, but I have some friends here, and I needed to take care of some business concerns. I was just about to visit you."

"Come and meet my new wife."

Stanton noticed a slight hesitation in his brother-in-law, but he followed along.

"Nice to meet you, madam," Horace said after Stanton made the introductions.

"The pleasure is mine, Mr. Sneed," Beth told him.

"It surprised me to learn you'd remarried," he said to Stanton.

"Yes, I'm sorry we didn't have time to invite you. Beth's father died soon after the wedding, or I would have written you."

"You're welcome to stay with us while you're in the area," Beth told Horace. "We'd enjoy your company."

"Thank you, but I'm visiting friends, and I don't plan to stay long. It's good to see you, Stanton." Horace shook his hand and left.

It was good to see Horace again, too. Stanton was glad Horace got to meet Beth, but he had mixed feelings about him staying at their house. On one hand, he would have enjoyed visiting with Horace, but on the other hand, he liked the privacy he and Beth shared. That didn't matter now, though, since Horace would be staying with another friend.

"What did the sheriff say?" Beth asked on the way home.

"He's going to get some men together and look for Ralph, but he doesn't think he's been in town since Saturday. If nothing turns up around here, he'll check in other towns."

"Mr. Sneed seemed nice, but I sensed him reserved upon meeting me."

"He's a good man, and although he didn't want me to marry his sister at first, he's always seemed to like me. We became pretty good friends. I'm surprised he didn't let me know he was in Middleville as soon as he arrived. He used to visit at the farm when he came to the area, and Molly and I sometimes went to Philadelphia around Christmas."

"Do you think he liked me?"

"Who wouldn't? You're a very likable person." *Too likable, if Ralph and Cecil were any indication.*

She gave him an amused smile. "I think you might be a bit biased."

"I can't deny it. I am very partial to your many charms." He couldn't contain his wide grin.

Thursday morning the sheriff and some men brought Ralph back. He had been shot. One of the men had ridden into town for the doctor, and others carried Ralph and put him on his bed.

Stanton felt shocked and confused. Why would someone shoot an indentured servant? If Ralph had any enemies, Stanton wasn't aware of it. He had been found on Stanton's property but not near the house or fields.

Ralph looked pale, blood-soaked, and bruised. He had been shot in the upper arm. The best Stanton could tell, no bones were shattered, but the ball had done a lot of damage to the flesh. He moaned at times, but otherwise he didn't seem to be aware of much.

"Was Ralph giving you any trouble?" the sheriff asked Stanton.

"No, why?'

"Ralph came to the tavern Saturday night, and he said you were jealous of him for no reason. Has Ralph been causing any problems with your wife?"

"He's watched her at times, but he's never been forward or said anything he shouldn't. Why do you ask?"

"I'm trying to figure out who had a reason to shoot him."

"Surely you don't think I shot my own servant."

"Stranger things have happened, but I'm not accusing you of anything. I'm just asking questions."

The doctor washed off the dried blood and wrapped Ralph's arm. He left some medicine with instructions regarding when to give it and told Beth to get as much broth and liquids into him as she could.

When everyone left, Stanton realized he and Beth were left to nurse Ralph back to health. With the wheat harvest soon upon them, he would also need all the help he could get on the farm. He didn't know how they would manage.

Stanton put out word he wanted to hire some extra help for harvest, but no one came for the job. Although some masters hired out their servants from time to time, they usually needed them during harvest time. The other farmers also often hired extra hands for the harvest, so there were few other men to be had. He might have found someone if he had time to go farther out in the colony, but he couldn't spare the time for that trip. He was already running later than he liked with the harvest.

Chapter Thirteen: The Harvest

"He reserveth unto us the appointed weeks of harvest."

—Jeremiah 5:34

Stanton hated that Beth had to care for Ralph. She had enough to do without being responsible for the bondservant, and Stanton didn't like it that they were in each other's company so much. At first, Ralph lay too sick and weak to notice her, but as he gained more strength, Stanton felt the man took advantage of her. He tried to keep her in his cabin as much as possible. Stanton helped whenever he could, but without Ralph's help, he had a harder time getting the work done on the farm.

Even with the extra burden of Ralph, however, Beth still remained efficient. Stanton marveled at how she managed to get everything accomplished that she did. She did twice as much in a day as Molly ever had.

He had just started cutting the wheat, when he saw Beth come toward him. She wore her oldest dress, a large hat, and her work shoes. Without saying anything, she started gathering up the wheat into sheaves.

"What are you doing?" he asked her.

"You need some help. You can't do all this on your own, and I like working outside."

"Beth, you have more than enough to do without helping in the fields."

"If you don't mind eating simple meals during harvest, I don't mind working in the fields."

"What about Ralph?"

"He's getting better. I left him some food and water in the cabin, and I think he'll be able to take care of himself now."

Stanton reluctantly accepted her help. It amazed him how fast she worked.

He found he liked having her working beside him. She would look up and smile at him, and his day brightened. She seemed to anticipate what he needed, and they made a good team. He considered again getting an indentured servant to help in the house, so Beth could work with him more. It would be hard to find someone who cooked as well as she did, though.

Even with Beth helping, the work went much slower than Stanton would have liked. Beth drove the team and wagon for Stanton to load the sheaves; then they took them to the barn. They would store the wheat in the barn and process it later, when they'd harvested all the crops. The wheat would need to be threshed, either by trampling or flailing to get the chaff off.

The following week, Ralph decided he would be able to drive the wagon. Stanton suspected he wanted to be close to Beth again, but it did make the process go faster.

"I notice you don't plant any rye," Beth said.

"I don't. I haven't acquired a taste for rye bread, and I try not to furnish grains to the liquor industry. Do you want me to start planting some next year?"

"No, I don't care for it either, and I respect you for not selling it to make whiskey. I just knew most farmers planted it in November so the crop would be ready to harvest with the wheat."

"You're right, but I just sow the wheat in September so it'll be ready in July. As you can see I also plant summer grains, like oats, corn, buckwheat, and a little barley, and we'll harvest them too."

"Stanton, Stanton." He awoke to Beth shaking his shoulder. "I smell smoke."

He smelled it too. The air hung thick with smoke, and the faint orange glow told him of a blaze. He hurried into his pants and shirt, and then rushed down the stairs. Beth followed right behind him.

He saw the burning wheat field immediately, and despair nearly overwhelmed him, as he ran to grab some buckets to fill in the springhouse. Beth followed him with two blankets she wet.

Stanton didn't take time to assess the situation. He just began fighting the fire with everything he had in him. The dry wheat burned fast.

Ralph came running to help. He used one hand to carry buckets of water to Stanton from the springhouse. Beth used a wet blanket to beat at the flames, and Stanton did likewise between pouring the buckets. He splashed one of the buckets on Beth's skirt. He wanted to make sure her clothing didn't catch on fire.

Suddenly he felt a wind come up, and it pushed the fire to the area they'd already cut. Maybe they'd be able to save the rest of it. When lightning flashed, thunder growled, and a heavy rain began, Stanton sighed. Nature put out the fire more quickly than he ever could.

"Thank you, Lord," he heard Beth whisper.

He thanked God for the rain too. He had lost some of the wheat, but not nearly as much as it could have been.

"Do you think the fire started from a lightning strike?" Beth asked.

"I guess it could have, but I didn't see any until just before the rain came, and I would've thought a lightning bolt would have hit one of the trees before it hit the wheat field."

"Look," Ralph said. He picked up a charred lantern in the field. "Do you think this could have started it?"

"It may have."

"That means someone intentionally started the fire." Beth's voice trembled.

They walked back to the house, and Ralph went to his cabin. His servant seemed to be recovering quickly. The wound hadn't been as bad as they'd first thought.

"I wonder what's going on," Stanton said. "First, the chicken heads, then Ralph getting shot, and now this. I can't imagine who'd do such things. Do you think Cecil is capable of this?"

"No, I don't. I think it's just as logical to blame the Widow Knotts as to accuse Cecil."

Stanton hadn't considered the widow at all. "I can't see her doing any of this. She'd never handle severed chicken heads, and I doubt if she knows how to shoot a gun. Neither would she come out here in the dark to start a fire. No, I think the culprit has to be a man."

"Perhaps the widow has a man working with her. Why are you accusing Cecil when you have no evidence at all? Is it because you don't like him?"

"I'm not accusing Cecil. I'm just trying to consider who might possibly hold a grudge. Why are you so quick to come to his defense? He did threaten you, when he said you'd regret rejecting his despicable offer, and he's the only person I can connect a motive to."

"Perhaps I come to Cecil's defense because you are so quick to point a finger at him. I'm certain that I'm no favorite of Widow Knotts. She'd set her cap for you, Stanton, and I think she's use to getting her way. I think we have just as much reason to suspect her as to suspect Cecil."

"Fiddlesticks! A man is much more likely to be involved in such mischief than a woman."

"And a jealous woman is much more dangerous than a jealous man." Beth's face had taken on a stubborn streak that he had rarely seen in her.

He hadn't intended to start an argument. He should have kept his thoughts to himself, but why did she always jump to defend Cecil? It rankled him to no end.

He sucked in a deep breath. "Come, we're both tired," he told her. "Let's go in and get cleaned up."

She turned to walk beside him, but when he put his hand on her back, he could feel her stiffen. He felt a sharp pain in his hand where her hair touched it and pulled it back. She looked at him.

"Your hands are burned," she said.

Stanton looked down at his hands. He hadn't noticed them during the fire, but now he felt their sting. "Maybe a little, but they're not bad."

"Come, let me tend to them."

Her concern made him feel better. He walked with her to the house. His hands had some blisters on top, but his palms weren't burned. Good, he would still be able to work tomorrow.

In the morning, they could tell more about the fire. It had burned about a twelve-foot area of the field, but

Stanton knew they were lucky it hadn't been more. They needed to hurry and get the rest of the wheat in before anything else happened.

Sunday, standing in the churchyard after the service, Stanton told the sheriff about the fire and the lantern. He gave Stanton a strange look.

"Trouble seems to be following you lately. Do you have any idea who might be doing this?"

"None at all." Stanton knew he'd better keep his suspicions about Cecil to himself until he had some proof.

Stanton turned away from the sheriff to find Beth talking with Cecil in front of the church. He gritted his teeth and hurried toward them with a determined stride.

"I burned my hand trying to catch a falling candle at the house," he heard Cecil say. "You can ask my parents if you don't believe me. It was stupid of me really, but I reacted before I thought."

Beth looked uncertain, and Stanton didn't know if Cecil had told the truth or not. He walked up to stand beside Beth. "Are you ready to go in, darling?" He wanted to get her away from Cecil, regardless.

"Yes."

She smiled at him and stepped closer, and Stanton wondered if she liked it that he hadn't made an issue of Cecil's burned hand. It did look suspicious, but he needed to proceed with caution. He'd look bad if he said anything now or acted in haste.

"Did I see Cecil Shippen with a burn on his hand?" the sheriff asked. Stanton hadn't realized he'd come up behind them. He seemed suspicious of Shippen, too.

"You did," Beth answered, "but he said he burned it on a candle at his house."

"Well, I'll look into that." His face held a determined look.

Good. Let the sheriff be the one to check it out.

They finished the wheat harvest the next week. Stanton would never have been able to get it in before fall without Beth's help. He hesitated to feel his crops were safe, however, because it would be just as easy to burn down the barn and everything in it. That would be a disaster, and he wouldn't allow himself to dwell on the possibility of someone setting fire to the house. He could do little, except be vigilant and pray.

Stanton found himself praying more now than ever. Somehow Beth had managed to turn him back toward God. She hadn't said anything about it, but he knew she lived her life close to God, and she expected him to do so too. He wanted to please her, and he wanted to be a better man for her. He sensed she had a strength of spirit that came from a higher power, and he wanted that back in his life. Fear of what might happen gripped him, and he knew he needed divine help. He could do so little to protect the farm or Beth. He needed God.

As soon as they had the wheat in, Beth started picking blackberries before they vanished. She'd missed the first of them, but she gathered all she could find.

Stanton tried to go with her, as often as he could. With all that had been happening, it made him nervous for her to be away from the house and out of sight for long periods of time. Besides, Beth had worked hard to help him in the fields, so it seemed only right for him to lend her a hand.

Helping Beth pick the berries also nurtured the closeness they shared. Their difference of opinion about Cecil had tried to drive a wedge of uncertainly between them, and Stanton hated that. But here, standing near each other for hours, filling buckets with blackberries and talking with ease, brought them closer again.

He looked over at her as she deftly maneuvered around the prickly briars. She looked so pretty no matter what she wore or what she was doing.

He looked at her trim waist and wondered when she would tell him she expected a child. He knew it was too early yet, but he kept hoping it would be soon. Even a girl might be all right, if she would work in the fields like her mother.

Beth looked over at her husband as he struggled to remove a pesky blackberry briar from his shirtsleeve. He remained a wonder to her. *Her husband.* She kept repeating the phrase to herself, hoping it would quit being so unbelievable. Even in her dreams, she could never have imagined that she could love someone as much as she did Stanton, but things between them were not perfect.

For one thing, Cecil still came between them. Beth knew Stanton resented her childhood friend. Maybe she should view his jealousy as flattering, but she didn't. She saw it as a lack of trust, and that bothered her.

The strange incidents also made matters more difficult. Stanton hadn't said anything, but she knew he worried about what might happen next, and she could understand. Someone had invaded their home to leave the severed chicken heads. Although the act must have been intended just to scare them, it also warned them someone wished them ill.

Even more unsettling—someone had shot Ralph, which showed how dangerous the culprit could be. Stanton said the two incidents might not be related, but Beth knew he didn't believe that. With the burning of the wheat field, Beth felt sure someone meant them harm.

She also worried that the person who shot Ralph had intended to shoot Stanton instead. Of course, by shooting the bond servant, the burden of bringing in the wheat harvest fell on Stanton alone, but she still feared for her husband's safety.

In addition, Beth felt sure the distressing episodes weren't over. Stanton and she both lived with the tension of wondering what would happen next.

The last thing that troubled her had nothing to do with outsiders. Stanton had never told her that he loved her. That couldn't be normal for a couple so recently married. Didn't men say it to women they courted or husbands tell it to their wives? Beth could feel his love in the way he treated her and in their intimate moments, but she still needed to hear him say it.

Stanton picked up the bell he'd ordered from the foundry and erected it in the backyard of the house. It wasn't a large one, but its ring could be heard throughout the farm, and, considering all that had happened, it did make Beth feel more secure.

"Don't panic if I ring the bell," Beth told him. "If we have visitors, it will be the best way to get you in from the fields."

Ralph's arm had healed well enough for him to help in the fall harvest. Beth still helped on many days, however, and she felt Stanton had grown to appreciate her working beside him. Actually, it gave her great pleasure to do so. Still, the worrisome situations remained unsolved and hung over them like dark foreboding clouds.

Chapter Fourteen: Gossip and Gunshots

"A great talker may be no fool but he is one that relies on him."

—Poor Richard's Almanack

"Have you heard the latest rumor?" Mistress Denny asked as Stanton and Beth parked the wagon to go to church.

"We try not to participate in gossip," Stanton told her softly. Beth could tell he wanted to take the sting out of his words.

"Well, you need to hear this. I'm not telling a soul but you. I doubt the truth of it, but you need to know what some folks are saying about you. They're saying Fiona Fletcher went to her aunt's home in Boston because she was in a family way and that you're the father. I thought it would be better to warn you, before you or Beth heard it unprepared."

"That's preposterous!" Stanton exclaimed.

Beth saw the shock on Stanton's face, but did it come from the untruth of the rumor or from being found out? Beth knew well how controlling Fiona could be. She also recognized how much physical beauty the spoiled young lady possessed. Hadn't she always wondered why Stanton chose her over Fiona? She had believed that Stanton didn't care for Fiona, but the accusations were mounting.

The rumor had several cracks in it, however. Beth knew how much Stanton wanted a son, and, if Fiona had carried his child, he would have married her right away. A man like him always met his responsibilities. In addition, Cecil had told her Fiona said the child was his, and that made more sense. Yet, the doubts wanted to hound Beth. Why did human nature always tend to believe the worst?

"I figured as much," Mistress Denny said, "but I thought you should know. I can't find the source of the rumor, but something like that spreads faster than spilled milk."

"Thank you, Mistress Denny. Please do what you can to dispel the gossip."

"I'll do that."

Stanton looked at Beth. "You believe me, don't you? I never saw Fiona alone. The only contact I had with her was when you were nearby, and when I ate dinner at the Fletchers the one time. I promise you I never touched her."

He looked directly into her eyes, and Beth saw a look of honesty and sincerity. She had no reason to doubt him. Hadn't he shown her over and over again how much he cared for her?

"I do believe you, Stanton." She put her hand on his arm and felt the tension leave him.

"Thank you," he whispered. He kissed her cheek and put his arm around her waist to pull her closer as they walked to the church.

Beth tried to lose herself in the service and worship, but it felt as if a hundred eyes were on them. Stanton took her hand in his and slipped them under the folds of her skirt to be less obvious. The way he always wanted to comfort and support her pleased her to no end. She wished she could lean into him and rest her head on his shoulder, but she knew that would be improper. Instead, she gave Stanton a smile of appreciation, sat straighter, and faced the preacher. Today, she appreciated the fact more than ever that Stanton had decided to come to the Presbyterian church where they could sit side by side.

When the service ended, Stanton led her out ahead of most of the people. She felt their stares, however. The minister greeted them as always. They were rushing for their wagon, when the oldest Durk child came running up.

"Papa said to ask you to dinner," he told them.

Stanton looked at her to see what Beth wanted to do. She felt torn. She knew the Durks would be good to confide in, but she felt the need to be home.

"Could we plan to eat with them next week instead?" she asked Stanton.

He nodded. "Tell your parents that we need to go home today," Stanton told the child, "but let them know we'll plan to come next Sunday, unless they tell us otherwise."

"I'm sorry about all this," Stanton said as they rode home.

"You don't need to apologize. You did nothing wrong, and you can't be held responsible for vicious gossip."

"I'm thankful you understand, but I wish I could spare you any worry or difficulty. There's been too much of those lately. I just wish we could find who's behind it all."

"Do you think the same person who started the rumors created the other problems?"

"I don't know, but it makes sense."

"Do you think it has something to do with our getting married? You didn't have problems like this until you brought me here, did you?"

"If it does, it's probably because someone is jealous."

Was he hinting that it must be Cecil again? She knew Cecil wasn't jealous of her, and he wouldn't take the time to pull such stunts. He was too busy courting half of the unmarried young women in the area. She wanted to tell Stanton what she thought, but she felt it would be better to not get into that discussion again.

"Did I ever tell you that Fiona approved my calling on her just after I started courting you? I told her father I had started seeing someone else and it held great promise."

"No, you didn't tell me. Do you think Fiona or her father may have started the rumors?"

"I briefly considered it, but I doubt he would do something like that. I can't see him starting a rumor that would disparage his daughter's reputation, and the same goes for Fiona."

She could tell Stanton's mind kept returning to Cecil. She had to admit he seemed the most likely suspect, if one looked at things in a rational manner.

"Did the sheriff investigate Cecil's burn as he said he would?"

"Yes, but Cecil's parents also claimed he burned his hand when a candle fell at their house. Are you beginning to doubt Cecil too?"

He gave her a teasing smile, but she wondered, if underneath, he was serious. She didn't know quite how to answer him, so she chose to be honest.

"No, I'm not, but I could be wrong. I know he appears to be the best suspect, but I've known him for a long time, and I can't see him being involved in something like this. If it involved doing a woman wrong, I would have no problem believing it, but this is not like Cecil. I can't help but believe there's someone else out there, someone we're missing."

"I like your honesty, Beth. I'm thankful you don't try to hide things from me, and you reveal your thoughts. Perhaps you're right. There could very well be someone we haven't thought about yet. Until he was shot, I considered it might be Ralph, but he wouldn't shoot himself. You don't have any other ideas, do you?"

"None whatsoever, except I'm looking forward to getting home. I think we should eat and perhaps take a nap. This has been a tiring day."

He looked at her carefully with a question in his eyes. She lifted her hand and stroked his cheek, then moved closer to him.

"Sometimes only you know how to comfort me," she told him.

His face softened with a smile. He put his arm around her and pulled her close.

"I love to comfort you," he said with a gleam in his eyes. "I'm so glad you married me."

People had started coming out of the Lutheran church when Stanton and Beth made their way to the Durks' house for dinner.

"Oh, Stanton," the Widow Knotts called as she tried to catch up to them.

Stanton muttered something under his breath that Beth couldn't hear. She knew he wanted to avoid Mistress Knotts.

"I heard you've been seeing Fiona Fletcher in secret. I could have entertained you much better."

"Mistress Knotts! You overstep the bounds of propriety. How dare you make such an underhanded proposition to me, and in front of my wife to boot. You should also know better than to listen to rumors."

Beth felt as shocked as Stanton sounded. What was this woman thinking?

"Oh, I'm sorry, Stanton. You're right. I should have said that when we're alone."

"No, madam. You shouldn't have said it at all, and I have no intention of ever being alone with you."

"Careful, Stanton. I'm not a person you want working against you. Perhaps we can talk later."

Stanton didn't answer her. He'd grown pensive and pale, so Beth put her hand on his arm to distract him.

"What are you thinking?" she asked after the widow had walked away.

He looked at her, and his eyes softened. "How much I dislike that woman and wish she would stay away from me. Her last comment also puzzled me. Now, I'm also beginning to think I should add her to the list of suspects. I suppose she could have someone working with her like you said." He shook his head.

"Come, let's go to dinner and forget what's happened for a while. At least the Durks are good friends."

"I'm going to the wooded area to search for grapes and nuts today," Beth told Stanton after breakfast. "With September already here, the grapes should be ready."

"I'd rather you wait until I can go with you. I dare not leave the corn harvest today, but we'll have it all gathered soon."

"I'd like to go several times. You and I can go later, but I missed part of the blackberries, and I don't want most of the grapes to be gone."

"Promise me you won't go deep into the forest, and you won't dally but will hurry back. With all that's been happening, I'll worry while you're gone."

"I promise, but I'm sure I'll be fine."

"Let me know when you get back."

"All right, but don't worry. I have a stew simmering, and I plan to be back in plenty of time for dinner."

Beth walked through the forest with a bucket in each hand. Stanton had said to not dally, but she wanted to take her time and enjoy the beautiful day. The forest almost seemed enchanted, and it refreshed her.

She found enough wild grapes to quickly fill one of her buckets, and in about a week, more would be ripe. She started filling the other bucket with black walnuts and chestnuts. They were just beginning to ripen and fall, and there'd be more of them later too. Once the bucket brimmed with nuts, she turned to go back to the house. Wouldn't Stanton be glad she'd returned so quickly?

Beth heard a squirrel playing around in the walnut tree, and a few more nuts fell to the ground. She started to bend over to pick them up, when she heard an explosion, felt something hit her head, and had a sense of falling.

By the position of the sun, it had to be dinnertime, and Beth hadn't come to tell Stanton she'd gotten back.

Had she misunderstood or forgotten? It would be unusual for her to do either.

They quit work and went to the house. The stew pot still sat near the fire, but he could find no sign of Beth.

Stanton's blood ran cold and his body felt like lead. *Please God, no!* His brief plea calmed him enough to get a coherent thought, but his heart raced so fast it ached.

"Do you think she might be lost in the woods?" Ralph asked as his face crinkled in worry.

"It's possible, but I doubt it. Beth has a very good sense of direction, and she promised she wouldn't go far. Let's go look for her. You take the east section of woods, and I'll search the west. Keep calling to her. Take your rifle and fire it if you find her. I'll do likewise."

Stanton chose the west section because he guessed at the direction she would have likely gone. He ran toward the forest with a whispered prayer on his lips.

"Dear God, please don't let anything happen to Beth. Keep her safe, I pray. She's so devoted to Thee, and she's helping to strengthen my faith. I desperately need her. Please let her be all right, and help me to find her quickly. I pray this in Jesus' name. Amen."

"Beth! Beth!" He'd cried her name until his throat hurt, but he'd seen no sign of her. He heard a rustle in the leaves and ran in that direction, but all he saw was a squirrel playing on the ground, and it scampered up a walnut tree when Stanton approached.

Then, he saw her. She lay crumpled on the ground, and his heart stopped. At the same time, his feet carried him forward, as if they knew what to do apart from him. He couldn't think. He couldn't breathe.

He shot his rifle into the air to let Ralph know that he'd found Beth, and then he scooped her up with care and put his ear to her chest. Her loud heartbeat quieted his terror, but his blood still raced and his mind panicked. He noticed her hair caked with blood. It had dried, and her hair had matted together so that he couldn't see how badly she'd been hurt. At least the bleeding had stopped, but he could still smell the sickening sweet metallic scent of it.

The squirrel sat on a high branch chattering away to him. "Thank you, little guy, for directing me to Beth."

His thoughts were mixed and confused, but he knew one thing for sure. Someone had intentionally harmed Beth, and it had to stop. He had just cleared the forest when she roused.

Chapter Fifteen: Recovering

"Sin is not hurtful because it is forbidden but it is forbidden because it's hurtful."

—Poor Richard's Almanack

"Stanton?"

"Yes, darling."

"My head hurts. What happened?"

"I don't know. I found you on the ground under a walnut tree in the forest."

"Put me down, and I'll walk."

"Not yet. We'll be home soon, and I'm going to put you to bed and send for the doctor."

"No, don't do that. I'm okay, and all he'll do is bleed me."

"Shhh, don't worry. I'll be able to tell more about what you need when I get you home."

Stanton could tell Beth had lost enough blood already, so he didn't think the doctor would bleed her. He'd feel better if she had the doctor's care.

He saw Ralph in the distance as he carried Beth into the house. When Ralph saw them, he came quickly.

Stanton climbed the steps to their bedroom and gently laid Beth in the bed. He got a basin of water and cloth and began to wash away some of the blood so he could see the wound. He tried to be as careful as possible to keep her head from starting to bleed again.

Ralph called out, and then rushed up the stairs. "How is she?"

"She has a head wound. I think you should ride for the doctor."

"No!" Beth proclaimed. "I don't need a doctor." She'd had her eyes closed, and Stanton had thought she'd fallen asleep.

He found a gash on the crown of her head. It looked raw and ugly but didn't look deep.

"How do you feel?"

"Not my best. I have the worst headache ever. I need a strong lavender tea. If you don't have any, you can send Ralph to town to buy some. It should help my pain."

"You have a gash on your head. I think the doctor should look at it."

Stanton glanced to the side at Ralph standing against the door facing. At least he hadn't completely entered the bedroom, and he remained quiet.

"How deep is it? Does it need stitching?" Beth didn't sound nearly as worried as him.

Stanton examined the wound more carefully. "It doesn't look deep, but it's very raw looking. It could become infected."

"Put some marigold cream on it to keep infection down and then some comfrey ointment to promote healing."

"Do you remember what happened?"

Beth rubbed her forehead. "I had filled my buckets with grapes and nuts. A squirrel knocked a few more walnuts from the tree, and I bent over to get them too, when I heard a blast. I felt something hit my head, and it caused me to fall. I think I might have been shot."

Stanton felt cold all over. He couldn't stand the thought of someone trying to kill Beth.

"Did anyone fetch my buckets?"

"No. I was too worried about you to even notice your buckets. I left my rifle there too. I'll send Ralph to get everything, but first let me see if we have the medicines you want. If not, I'll also send him to Middleville."

"I think that little squirrel may have saved my life. If he hadn't knocked some more nuts down from the tree, I wouldn't have been bending over, and the shot would have hit me squarely."

Stanton sat down in a chair beside the bed. His legs had suddenly grown too weak to stand.

"That squirrel may have saved you a second time. The noise from one scampering about in the leaves drew me to you."

When he gained enough strength back, Stanton went downstairs and found the lavender and the marigold cream. Beth assured him they could wait on the comfrey ointment. He tried to apply the cream to her wound without hurting her, and, following Beth's directions, he made her the medicinal lavender tea, which she said would help relieve her headache.

"I found a rifle ball lodged in a tree," Ralph said when he returned with Stanton's rifle and Beth's buckets. "I didn't bother it in case you want to send for the sheriff."

"I'll have you go in tomorrow morning. I'll write the sheriff a report you can give him of what happened. You can also pick up some comfrey ointment from the doctor's apothecary shop for Beth."

Stanton and Ralph ate some of the stew for a late dinner. Stanton managed to get Beth to drink some of the broth from a cup, but she said it hurt her head to sit up.

He sent Ralph back out to the field, but he stayed with Beth. He wanted to be near her.

Thank Thee, Lord, for sparing Beth. Please help her to heal well without any complications. I thank Thee with all my heart for leading me to her and for keeping her from being killed. Help me to be the man she needs me to be, and help us find out who's doing this. Keep us safe, I pray. Amen.

"Would you like me to sleep in the other room tonight?" he asked her at bedtime. "Do you think my moving around might bother you?"

"No. I'll sleep better with you beside me."

When Stanton lay down surrounded by the darkness, fear gripped him, as he thought of how close he'd come to losing Beth today. Something had to be done to stop this madness before someone ended up dead. He had to find this unknown shadow and bring it to light.

Until today, he'd considered Cecil the main suspect, but he didn't think Cecil would try to kill Beth. Who could it be, then? Whoever it was seemed to hold ill feelings against Beth, and possibly Ralph, since they'd both been shot. Could Agnes Knotts be the one behind it after all?

"It's all right, Stanton." Beth reached over and took his hand. "I'm still here, and I'm going to be fine."

How could she know what he felt without even asking? He squeezed her warm hand. What would he have done if he'd lost her? It might be better never to have met her than to know such happiness and have it ripped away. But Beth was right. She had been spared. He should focus on the blessings and pray. He would pray incessantly, just as the Bible said, that the culprit would be caught before he or she did any more damage.

"Trust the Lord to protect us." She pulled closer into him. "We can't do it ourselves, but He can. Believe that He will. In Proverbs it says, 'The fear of man bringeth a snare; but whoso putteth his trust in the Lord shall be safe.'"

"I'm trying." He kissed her hand.

"If you will put it all in His hands, you won't have to worry. He's much more capable of handling it than we are."

"My head knows that, but my heart is having a hard time moving beyond the fear of losing you."

"I would be devastated too, if I lost you, but I'm not letting myself think like that. I'm trusting God to take care of us both."

Stanton realized his faith had never been as strong as Beth's. Strange how he'd grown up going to church, but until he married Beth, he'd never know what faith entailed. He'd always tried to take care of any situation himself. Giving everything to God seemed too difficult, and he wondered if he'd ever be able to do it, but he sensed he needed to.

"I feel much better this morning," Beth told him as she started to sit up.

"I'm glad," he told her as he gently pushed her back down, "but I still want you to stay in bed today. I'm capable of getting my own meals. After all, I'd been doing so for months before I married you. I'll fix you some more lavender tea, if you need it, bring you some bread and jam, and put some more marigold cream on your head."

"I'll let you do all that, if you'll go out and do the farm work today. I don't need you sitting here with me, despite the fact I enjoy your company so much. I know you have things you need to take care of."

"If you're sure? You can always ring the bell if you need me. I still insist that you stay in bed. I don't want you taking a fall on top of everything else. I'll come back to check on you along."

The next day, Stanton came back for dinner to find Beth in the kitchen. Not only had she fixed dinner, she stood before the fireplace making grape jelly.

"Beth, I thought I told you to stay in bed. What are you doing?"

"I didn't want the grapes to spoil, and I do feel so much better. My headache has almost disappeared, I'm not dizzy at all, and my strength has returned."

"What am I going to do with you?"

"Oh, I can think of a few things."

He laughed in spite of himself. He loved it when she acted the coquette with him. She gave him a suggestive smile, and he melted. She knew how to sway him, the little imp.

"Come here."

He put his arms around her and kissed her forehead. He was still holding her when Ralph came in. He didn't move away quickly and neither did Beth. Good. Let Ralph see where her heart lay.

Stanton decided to come back to the house to check on Beth midafternoon. Knowing that she'd worked all morning, he feared she might continue to overdo things.

She had finished the jelly and left the two crocks sitting on the table to cool. He tiptoed up the stairs and found her in the bedroom sleeping. He smiled to himself, pleased that she'd finally done what he wanted. He went back downstairs and started back to the fields, when Ralph and the sheriff rode up.

"Your letter sounded serious," the sheriff said. "It looks like the trouble is getting worse."

"It does, and, I admit, I'm worried. This looks like attempted murder, and I can't lose my wife."

"I understand. That's why I'm here. Let me look around and see if I can come up with anything."

Stanton showed the sheriff where he'd found Beth. The man looked around, noted the dried blood, and dug the rifle ball out of a tree with his knife. He determined the direction from where he thought the shot came and asked Stanton to help him look around that area.

"Don't move anything you find but call me," he told Stanton.

The sheriff found a scrap of cloth snagged on a bush in a thicket. It appeared to be made of manufactured cotton and not homespun, which seemed unusual. Most people around here made their cloth and clothing. Did that mean the person they were hunting didn't live here? Of course, some people, like Cecil Shippen and the Fletchers, had more expensive clothing. Others, like Stanton, had some finer clothing for Sunday and special occasions. What about the Widow Knotts? He guessed she had some of both too.

"Well, this is not much," the sheriff said, "but it's the first two pieces of concrete evidence we have. Let's go back. I'd like to talk to Beth."

Stanton smiled when he saw Beth sitting at the kitchen table. He didn't like the idea of leading the sheriff to their bedroom. She looked much better than she had yesterday, although her hair was still dotted with some of the dried blood. She looked at the sheriff with a mixture of anticipation and dread.

"I need to ask you a few questions, Mistress Klein," the sheriff said. "Tell me what you remember about the shooting yesterday. Take your time, and give me all the details you can."

"Would you like some tea or apple cider, while we talk?" she asked him.

"No, thank you."

Beth told him the same thing she'd told Stanton. The sheriff's attention never left Beth, and he inserted a few questions along.

"May I also see the wound on your head?"

Being as gentle as he could, Stanton moved Beth's hair aside so the sheriff could better look at the wound. When the sheriff left, he would apply the comfrey ointment Ralph had brought back, since Beth said the ointment would make it heal faster.

The following afternoon, Stanton helped Beth wash her hair. She insisted she could do it herself, but he wanted to help. It would be a tedious task to get the dried blood out without reopening the wound.

He sat her outside in a chair with her head back. The fall day had grown mild, and the sun warmed them. He wet her hair, lathered the tresses, rinsed, and repeated the process. He left the area around the wound alone but managed to get the blood washed from the rest of her hair. He first used his fingers to untangle the biggest snags. Then he followed Beth's advice and combed out the tangles beginning at the bottom and working up. Even after her hair hung tangle-free, he continued to comb it. He liked to feel her hair. Even in its damp state, it felt as soft as silk. She had fine hair, but she had a lot of it.

He also liked to watch her hair change colors in the light. As he moved it, it took on different hues with some darker and some lighter. Its richness fascinated him. He'd always thought he liked blond hair better, but nothing could be prettier than her deep-brown color that almost turned chestnut in the sun.

"Thank you," she told him. "You did a wonderful job."

"There's nothing to thank me for. I enjoyed playing with your hair."

She laughed. "You have my permission to do this any time you'd like. It's a luxury I haven't had since I was a little girl and my mother was alive."

Chapter Sixteen: Indians

"I expect to pass through life but once. If therefore, there be any kindness I can show, or any good thing I can do to any fellow being, let me do it now and not defer or neglect it, as I shall not pass this way again"

--William Penn

Stanton had been talking about the Indians in the area earlier that morning, and, as she went about her work, Beth's mind kept thinking about them. Stanton's farm no longer set on the western frontier, because other settlers had moved farther west, but the Indians could still pose a threat.

There hadn't been much trouble with the Indians in years, not since the disputes in 1728. It seemed to Beth that Pennsylvania had been blessed with peace more than any of the other colonies. William Penn had started a policy of talks and negotiations, and that policy had served them well over the years. When the Indians protested the settlers' constant pressure to settle farther and farther into their hunting lands, the colonial government tried to bargain and buy more land, but the Indians often got cheated, or so it seemed. The treaty signed two years ago was a good example.

The Delaware Indians agreed to sell all the land a colonist could walk through in a day and a half. Of course, the settlers chose their most able walkers, but they also used three men instead of one. As one man began to tire, a fresh one would take his place. In the end, Pennsylvania managed to claim a vast amount of the fertile Delaware land. This land came from their hunting grounds, which they had to have in order to survive. Even this couldn't satisfy the land-hungry settlers, however, and they continued to encroach on Indian land.

Beth decided to dip candles that morning. She had everything set up in the back yard but had gone into the house to stir the stew and rotate the spider with the cornbread. Everything seemed almost done. She'd just returned to the candles, when three Indian braves stood beside her. She hadn't heard a sound.

Her throat closed and her pulse quickened. She knew she stood at their mercy, for neither Stanton nor Ralph would hear her cries, and she would be unable to ring the bell. How long would it be before the men came in for dinner?

She wanted to back off, but memories from her childhood held her in place. "Stand your ground and show no fear," she heard her father say. "The Indians appreciate bravery." Of course, then, her father had been beside her, and it had been easier to be brave.

Beth continued to dip that round of candles. The Indians stood and watched, but they'd moved to the other side of the pot, and Beth felt more comfortable. She tried to glance at them and get a closer look as she worked. One was older and looked to be close to his middle years. The other two looked to be in their twenties.

When all the candles had been dipped one more time, she stopped and looked up, to see if she could determine what they wanted. The older one caught her eye, and she froze. A distant memory flitted and teased her.

"Okwes?" she asked.

He looked at her harder. *"Chemames?"*

She smiled with relief. Okwes had come to her father's farm needing food and water. She had been twelve at the time, and she had seen to his needs. Her father had been shocked to find the brave sitting under the shade tree eating part of their dinner Beth had given him, but the Indian had become a friend to them both. He had called her "rabbit" in his language.

"Yes." She nodded to him and smiled.

He mirrored her welcome and turned to talk to his companions in their language. They laughed at whatever he told them and looked back at her.

Okwes looked at her again, and Beth wondered if he would open his arms for her to rush into, as he had done each time he'd come after that first encounter. He didn't, however.

"Big Chemames," he said with a smile.

Yes, she had grown up. She guessed that meant she'd become too big to rush into his outstretched arms.

"Father?" Okwes asked.

"He died," Beth told him with a sad face.

"Dead?"

She nodded. Okwes slapped his chest, and she knew he was telling her he felt her sorrow.

"Are you hungry?" she asked as she motioned toward her mouth with her fingers.

Okwes shook his head. "Water," he said.

She brought them some water, and they drank it all. One of the younger men became interested in the bell.

He jiggled the clapper, and the bell rang. He jumped back, and Okwes laughed at him. The younger one smiled and rang the bell again and again.

Beth knew what would happen now. She hoped Stanton didn't start shooting before she could stop him. He had already told her that he hadn't seen Indians this close to Middleville for a long time.

She and the Delaware watched as Stanton and Ralph came into sight. They men paused to assess the situation, and Ralph started to raise his rifle. Stanton put his hand out and pushed the barrel down, but he hurried toward them with Ralph following.

As soon as Stanton came close, Beth moved to his side. He put his left arm around her shoulders but held his rifle ready in his right hand.

"This is Okwes, an old friend from my childhood," Beth told him. "He came to our farm after Mother died, and I fed him. Father couldn't believe it when he found an Indian sitting under a shade tree eating some of our dinner, but he became our friend. I haven't seen him in years."

"Welcome," Stanton said, but Beth could still feel his tension. He stood ready should trouble come.

"Your man?" Okwes asked.

"Yes. This is Stanton, my husband."

"Good. Chemames need man. No father."

"Would you like to eat with us?" Stanton asked. He had begun to relax some.

"No eat. We go." Okwes said. He turned to Beth. "Good see."

"It is so good to see you too," Beth told him. "Come again if you are in the area."

He nodded and turned to walk away. The other two followed him.

"I'm glad they left," Ralph said. Beth ignored him.

"I didn't know what to think when I saw you surrounded by three Delaware braves," Stanton told her. "I'm glad you rang the bell."

"I didn't ring it. One of Okwes's friends did. I think he liked it, although it startled him at first."

"I'm glad they were friendly. There've been some recent incidents in some other parts of the colonies. I think, as the population grows, relations with the Indians are going to get more tense."

"That makes sense, since we keep taking their lands," Beth said.

"I just hope it doesn't come to a war." Stanton rubbed the back of his neck. "I've heard that some of the French trappers to the north have been trying to stir up the Indians against us. Sometimes I think the French would like to have all this land for themselves."

"Well, that's never going to happen," Ralph said. "There aren't enough French here to fight the English."

"I wouldn't dismiss the danger," Stanton said. "If the Indians took the French side, they might have the advantage. Besides, in a war, soldiers from the Continent would probably be sent to aid both sides. That could make it a long fight."

"Do you think this will happen soon?" Beth asked.

"I don't think so," Stanton told her. "I hope not. I hope it doesn't happen at all."

"I think we should have wiped all the Indians out long ago," Ralph said. "That would have solved the problem."

Beth struggled to control her anger. "They're God's people too," she told him. "They were on the land first."

"But it's ours now. The Indians don't believe in God. They're savage heathens."

"Many have been converted, and they've always believed in a creator."

"The Indians don't believe in owning the land," Stanton said. "That's been part of their problem. They see the land as a resource put here for man's use. To most of them, owning land is as foreign as owning the wind or the air."

"But they don't understand the need to clear the land to farm," Ralph said.

"No," Beth agreed. "They see cutting trees and plowing the fields as desecrating the earth."

"I fear there's no easy solution," Stanton said. "Our ideas are too different. Next time though, Beth, I want you to ring the bell. Anytime men come to visit, you should call me in from the fields."

Her independent nature wanted to disagree, but she knew he was right. "I will," she agreed, "but today they were at my side before I knew it."

"Ralph seems very hard-hearted when it comes to the Indians," Beth said to Stanton as they lay in bed that night. "I'm glad you don't think like that."

"He's just expressing the same opinion that many of the colonists have. I just wish we could all get along without conflict, but that's hard when the two sides see things so differently. If war ever comes, though, I would feel compelled to support the colonies. I might have to fight against the Indians."

She took a deep breath. "I know. I understand that, but I pray we can remain at peace."

"So do I, but right now I'm more worried about whoever has tried to harm you. That's the more immediate threat."

Chapter Seventeen: The Bondswoman

"Let thy maid-servant be faithful, strong, and homely."

—Poor Richard's Almanack

Stanton walked with Beth into the forest. The grapes were gone for the season, but the nuts had become more numerous, and Beth could collect twice as many with him along. They stored the walnuts to crack later on winter days. He also went, because he wanted to protect her as much as he could.

He had most of the harvest in, and he found himself looking forward to spending more time with Beth. Whatever they did together turned into a time of fun. She injected enthusiasm, liveliness, and laughter into everything. She brought joy to his life. In fact, he had never been so happy in his entire life as when they were together. If only the dark cloud of someone trying to harm them didn't hang in the background.

Stanton and Beth made a trip to Middleville the following Wednesday to buy what they needed from the store. Beth then went to visit with Mistress Durk, while Stanton went to the blacksmith shop. He had just arrived at the shop, when he saw Molly's brother coming toward him.

"Stanton." Horace Sneed came hurrying into the shop. "I'm glad to see you. I had planned to ride out to your place, but you've saved me a trip."

"Good to see you too, Horace." Stanton put out his hand and they shook. "What can I do for you?"

"I wondered if I could interest you in a female servant. I won her in a card game, of all things, but I have a good housekeeper who wouldn't like me bringing her a servant without her say in it. This girl only has three more years on her indenture, so I'll sell her bond to you at a good price."

"I've been considering getting Beth some help. She likes to work outside as much as possible, and it would be good if she didn't have so much to do in the house."

"Come with me to the tavern, where we can sit and talk about it. I'll buy you an ale."

"I'll take some cider. Can I have a look at the woman?" Stanton wanted to assess whether or not the woman could be trusted and be helpful.

"This is Ida Loeffler," Horace said, nodding to an attractive young woman.

She didn't look Stanton in the eye, but he'd prefer she be shy rather than too bold. She appeared younger than him with blond hair and blue eyes. She was a comely young lady, and she looked fit.

"Do you know how to cook and tend house?" he asked, and she nodded.

"How old are you?"

"Twenty-three, sir," she answered in a thick German accent.

"How well do you speak English?"

His grandparents and father had spoken German fluently, but his parents had encouraged him to speak only in English, and he'd forgotten much of his German from lack of practice, especially in the time since they'd died.

"I'm learning fast. I've been here four years now."

They left Ida in Horace's wagon, and he and Horace went to the tavern, had their drinks, and struck a bargain. When they came out, Stanton put Ida in his wagon and drove back to the Durks. He couldn't wait to see Beth's surprise.

When he collected Beth and took her to his wagon, she looked surprised, all right. *Shocked* would have described her expression better.

"You bought a bondswoman?" she asked, and Stanton could tell by the tone of her voice she found no pleasure in his surprise.

"Yes, I know how you like gardening and working outside, so I thought it would be helpful to have someone to do most of the housework. To be honest, I liked having you help me with the harvest this year, but I don't want you overtaxed. I think you work too hard."

"I enjoy working on the farm, and I like taking care of your household. Besides, with winter coming, there won't be as much to do outside."

He explained how Horace Sneed had approached him about buying the woman's bond. Beth listened but said nothing.

Was that a look of hurt he saw in her face? Did she think he was trying to replace her? Heaven forbid! Nothing could be further from the truth. He had just wanted to help her and make life easier for her.

"Shall we go home? We can talk more about this later."

Beth nodded, and they made their way to the wagon. Ida had moved over on the wagon seat to sit in the middle, which would put her close to him. What could she be thinking? She hadn't sat that close when they'd come.

Stanton introduced the two women and helped Beth up on his side, so she'd sit in the middle, beside him. This forced Ida to slide over. Beth said little on the way home, so conversation lagged. Apparently Beth chose to remain silent, and with Ida's presence, he let her.

Stanton helped Beth down, but since Ida sat and waited, he then went to help her down too. As he lifted the servant down, she tripped and fell into him, and he had to put out his arms to steady her. He looked over to see Beth staring at them in disbelief.

Knowing the scene hadn't looked good, he went over, put his arm around Beth, and led her into the house. He hated the tension and stiffness he felt in her body. Ida followed along behind.

"Where are your things?" Beth asked the girl.

"I don't have any," Ida said as she hung her head. "My former mistress wouldn't let me take anything with me."

"Where shall I put her?" Beth asked Stanton.

He hadn't considered that. "Upstairs in the other bed chamber, I guess."

"Come," Beth told Ida. "I'll find you a bed gown and a change of clothes. I think we are close to the same size." She sounded resolved to the new situation but still unhappy about it.

"Thank you," Ida answered.

Her hips swayed as she climbed the stairs behind Beth, and she looked over her shoulder at him at the top of the stairs. What had he gotten himself into? He only agreed to take her on to please Beth.

He felt like a coward when he escaped to the barn, but he felt it would be better to let the women work things out. Stanton used to go to the barn often when he'd been married to Molly. He hadn't done that with Beth, because he enjoyed her company too much.

He returned to the house near suppertime, and Ida was in the kitchen cooking. Beth was nowhere in sight.

"Where's my wife?" he asked Ida.

"She went up to her room after showing me what she wanted me to do for supper."

Stanton climbed the steps and opened the bedroom door slowly, in case Beth had fallen asleep. She lay on the bed staring at the ceiling. Her eyes were moist and red, and he knew she'd been crying.

"Darling, what's wrong?"

He had to ask, although he knew the answer. His heart broke when she looked at him. How could trying to help cause her so much pain?

"I thought you liked my cooking and the way I took care of things." Her voice quivered as she tried to hold back more tears.

"I do, but I wanted to make things easier for you. I didn't want you to have to work so hard. Give Ida the tasks you don't like to do, and you do those things you like."

"I like it all."

"I don't think you enjoy the laundry. Let her do the washing and ironing."

"Stanton, we never wash clothes more often than once a week. I thought we agreed that I'd let you know if I ever wanted help. Have I let you know? I enjoy keeping everything in order here, and I've established a routine. I don't think there's enough to keep two women busy all the time, and I hate being idle. I like to stay busy because it makes me feel I'm accomplishing something. It makes me feel as if we're equal partners on the farm."

"I'm sorry, dear. The last thing I wanted to do is cause you distress. When Horace gave me the opportunity, you weren't there to ask about it. He presented me with a good deal, and I took it. Will you just give her a chance? Maybe things will work out better than you think."

"She's very pretty, and she's German."

"I hadn't noticed. No one could ever be as pretty to me as you are, and I've developed a certain fondness for the Welsh, especially a Welsh-German mix. I'm very happy you're my wife, Beth. Never doubt that. I would never look at another woman because, I'm not that kind of man and because I'm so satisfied with you."

She gave him a weak smile, and he took her in his arms. He kissed her with all the passion he felt for her, and she relaxed against him. As they went downstairs to supper, he found himself looking forward to tonight, when he planned to show her again how much she meant to him.

Ida prepared tasty food, but it didn't compare with what Beth cooked, and he planned to tell Beth so, when they were alone. When Ida served the plates or poured the drinks, she sided up too close to Stanton. He wondered at her intentions and could imagine what Beth must be thinking. Where was the shy servant he thought he'd purchased?

Beth looked at her husband across the table. She could tell he didn't think much of the supper Ida set before him, but he ate it and said nothing. Beth picked at her food. Her appetite had fled.

Despite Stanton's reassurances, she felt hurt. Why would he even consider buying the woman's indenture without talking with her? She knew many men made all the decisions without consulting their wives, but Stanton had never seemed to be that kind of man. Besides, she also knew most wives had more influence on their husbands than their men would admit.

She watched Ida rub up against Stanton as she served the meal. She could better understand how Stanton had felt when he saw Cecil's hand on her arm now. Jealousy coursed through Beth, and it seemed she could do little to stop it.

To give Stanton credit, he seemed more bothered or embarrassed by the flirtatious servant than enticed. He didn't show any interest. Was what he told Beth true? Did he see her as the only woman for him? That couldn't be right. What about Molly? Well, Molly wasn't here, but Ida flaunted her presence.

"You have a very handsome husband," Ida told Beth as they cleaned up after supper. Beth didn't like the interest she heard in the servant's voice.

"Yes, and he's devoted to me. I'm indeed blessed."

"Men were made to be unfaithful. One woman is never enough."

"You're wrong. God made Adam and Eve to be faithful to each other, but He gave them free will, and they chose to sin. Their ill-fated choice brought all kinds of sin into their lives and into the world."

"Well, that happened long ago, and just think of all the sin that's taken place since. I've always found men to have roving eyes, dirty minds, and wandering hands, which often lead to other things."

"Are you trying to tell me you're interested in my husband?" Beth knew she hadn't managed to hide the disgust or frustration in her voice.

"Perhaps I'm trying to tell you he's interested in me. Didn't you see him take me in his arms when he handed me down from the wagon?"

"I saw you fall into his arms."

"Who starts something doesn't really matter, does it? It's what happens and how it ends that's important."

"Don't push me, Ida, or try to seduce my husband. I can convince Stanton to get rid of you."

"But you won't, will you? If you do, you'll never be sure about him or be able to trust him. And, what's worse, he'd know you didn't trust him."

Beth looked at Ida, as the servant came in carrying a bucket. She had asked to go into the woods to see if she could find anything left to gather, and Beth had been glad to have some time to herself.

Things hadn't gotten any better. Ida still flirted with Stanton and flaunted herself at every opportunity. She needled Beth, as if she dared her to take action, and much of the joy went from Beth's life. She still liked being Stanton's wife, but there were no playful moments like they'd once shared. Beth felt weighed down with burdens placed on her by Ida.

"I will not serve these," Beth told Ida. "It's too dangerous."

"I know what I'm doing," Ida shot back as Stanton came into the kitchen.

"I don't like your tone of voice, Ida," he said. "What's going on?"

"I picked some mushrooms, but Mistress Klein refuses to cook them," Ida complained.

"Stanton, I know mushrooms," Beth told him, "but I rarely pick them because of the poisonous ones. If I do cook them, I only choose the varieties that aren't easy to mistake with a poisonous one. I can look at the ones Ida picked and know there are some lethal ones in the batch, and there are others I'm not sure of. I think it's safer to throw them all out."

"Then, we'll throw them out," Stanton said. "Ida, my wife is your mistress, and you're to do what she asks without arguing. I don't ever want to hear you use an ill tone with her again. Do I make myself clear? I'm considering selling your bond, as it is. You'd better not cause problems, and, while I'm trying to clear up matters, I don't like your flirty ways around me. It makes both me and Beth uncomfortable. You can either control yourself or you'll be gone."

"Yes sir." Ida looked contrite, but Beth couldn't be sure if that's how she really felt.

Beth looked at her husband anew. Without question, he'd always taken Beth's side in any disagreement with Ida. Just now he'd spoken to Ida in no uncertain terms. The situation couldn't be easy for him either, as he tried to diffuse circumstances, which seemed determined to explode. She just wished with all her heart that Stanton had never brought the woman here.

Beth did what she'd always done in difficult times—she took it to the Lord. She prayed over and over again for God to be ever present and to give them all peace. She also tried hard to treat Ida as she should, as a child of the Father, but she found it hard when the woman still tried to ensnare Stanton and treated Beth with some degree of contempt.

Chapter Eighteen: Couples

"Love, and be lov'd."

—Poor Richard's Almanack

Stanton watched Beth go through the days as if she had an unbearable weight on her shoulders. She rarely smiled and never laughed anymore. What had he done? He wanted the Beth back that he'd married. He'd wanted to make her happy, not sad. He intended to start looking for someone to buy Ida's bond.

He could understand how Beth felt. If Ralph, Cecil, or any other man had acted toward Beth the way Ida did him, he would be furious. Perhaps the only answer was to sell Ida's indenture to someone else.

He had to admire Beth. She never treated Ida with harshness or callousness, as he'd have been prone to do in her place. She might be aloof, but she never showed cruelty.

He knew Beth tried to give Ida chores and leave her to complete them, but they often still worked together on something, like making sauerkraut. Beth's cabbage had done well. She pulled four plants, roots and all, and hung them in the root cellar to use first. The sauerkraut took more work, but it would keep much longer.

Stanton could tell Beth didn't enjoy working with Ida. The servant had turned out to be much different than he expected. She seemed to look for ways she could cause conflict or problems, but she did the jobs assigned to her.

Ida brought one benefit Stanton hadn't considered. Ralph's attention turned from Beth to the new girl. Stanton hoped Ida would also focus on Ralph, but so far she still paid Stanton too much interest.

He found it odd that Ida tried to do inappropriate things even more often with Beth around. If the woman wanted to ensnare him, why would she act this way? Why didn't she try to keep her flirting a secret? He should have given it much closer consideration before agreeing to buy the woman's papers from Horace. He'd never dreamed she could complicate their lives so much. If he didn't find someone to buy her soon, he would have to let her go and count his loss. He just hated to put her out without any prospects. She could end up resorting to immoral ways to make her living, and he'd be partly responsible.

Stanton could tell Beth wanted to do what he'd asked and make Ida fit into the household, freeing up some time for her. Beth did all the cooking now, although she set Ida to doing some of preparation and cleanup. That suited him fine, because Beth's food tasted much better.

Beth also spent more time sewing now, since the harvest had been brought in. She altered some of the dresses from her mother's trunk, and she'd found some cloth there that she could use.

Stanton hated the fact that Ida stayed in the house. He hadn't considered that either, before he'd brought her home. He missed having Beth to himself most of the time they were inside. Even when they were in their bedroom, he could tell Beth tried to be quieter with Ida just across the hall. The bondswoman had put a damper on almost everything.

He'd learned one very important lesson. He needed to talk decisions over with his wife first. He sure hadn't thought things through when he decided to get Ida. Even if Beth had been more pleased with Ida, Stanton didn't think he would be. He longed for things to be back to the way they were before.

"Mr. Klein, could I talk with you?" Ralph asked later that day.

"Sure, Ralph. What is it?"

"I wanted to ask you not to sell Ida's papers and ask if you'd give me a chance to court her. I know neither she nor I are supposed to marry before our indentures are over, but we could with your permission, and I think it might solve a lot of our problems if she and I married. She could move into my cabin, and, since her period of servitude is longer than mine, you could pay me a wage for the year until she's free. She could help Mistress Klein as needed and take care of me and the cabin the rest of the time. What do you say?"

"You have my permission to court her, but you need to keep her from flirting with me. If Ida is agreeable, I'll sign for you two to marry with the condition that you serve out your indentures." Could this be the answer to his dilemma? He certainly hoped so.

At least the life-threatening incidents had ceased. Ida had taken the focus off that, and Stanton hoped they had truly stopped for good, but he reminded himself he still needed to be vigilant. Perhaps with winter here, when they all would be inside more, keeping an eye on Beth would be easier.

"Thank you, sir."

"Ralph, I want you to know I've felt as if Ida has been on the verge of asking me to take her into a barn stall when she's followed me outside sometimes. I won't have that. If you don't stop her wanton ways, I will sell her indenture. I want you to understand that."

Ralph's face turned redder than his hair and freckles. "I understand. I don't know what's going on, but I don't think that's her usual nature. Before I marry her, though, I'll make sure. And if I do marry her, I'm sure that won't be a problem. I'll see to it."

Beth seemed to like the idea, when Stanton told her of the conversation he'd had with Ralph. Perhaps this would prove to be the best solution of all.

"Did you know Ida has been hinting that you and she were having an affair?" Beth asked.

"No, why didn't you tell me? I hope you know that's not true. I'd have gotten rid of her if I'd known."

"I didn't believe it, and I didn't want you to get rid of her because of something I said. It's been your decision to get her, and I thought it should be your decision on whether or not she stayed. I could tell, when we were all together, that you didn't like her flirting. It almost reminded me of Sarah, Hagar, and Abraham in the Bible, where Hagar despised Sarah."

"I hope we don't remind you of that story. Hagar had Abraham's child, and there's no chance of that happening here. Has Ida been mistreating you?"

"Just in little ways. You heard her tone of voice that day with the mushrooms. She hasn't always been as respectful as she should be."

"If things don't get better after Ralph starts courting her, let me know. If she refuses Ralph, I will sell her indenture."

Stanton guessed Ralph and Ida must have had a long talk, because things did change. Ida accepted Ralph's courtship, and she seemed happier. She also quit flirting with Stanton—another blessing. Beth even said the servant had become more courteous with her.

Stanton and Ralph devoted much of October to gathering enough wood to see them through the winter. It required more than one month's work, but if they could get enough cut, they could add to it all along. With Beth cooking more than Stanton had last winter without Molly, it would take more firewood, and Stanton wanted to keep the house warmer for her too.

How strange that he'd first dreaded the thoughts of winter after the last one, but now that he had Beth, he eagerly looked forward to it. He wanted to snuggle close to her to stay warm through the night. He liked the idea of doing chores together, like cracking walnuts or threshing and winnowing the wheat. He looked forward to reading together by the firelight or playing chess as the wind howled outside. He smiled to himself. He just wanted to be near his wife and couldn't get enough of her.

He hoped the danger of someone harming her had passed, since there had been no further incidents. Yet, until they knew for sure, he still needed to stay alert. No matter how better things looked, that threat always lingered in the background, and Stanton prayed about it every day.

Before much of the winter had passed, he'd have Beth alone in the house once more. Ralph and Ida were planning a December wedding. Stanton couldn't wait.

It would be a small affair following the worship service at the Presbyterian church. Beth planned a dinner for the couple afterward with only a few people invited. They'd invite both ministers and their families, Mistress Denny, and the sheriff.

Beth had enthusiastically helped plan everything. Like Stanton, she felt Ralph and Ida had found what they needed in each other.

Stanton had mixed feelings about inviting the sheriff, but Beth felt it would be important to stay on friendly terms with him, and Stanton had agreed. There had been no news about who might have shot Beth or done any of the other things. Stanton hoped to draw the sheriff off to the side at the dinner and find out how his investigation progressed. He had been talking with him every chance he got.

Stanton and Ralph came in from gathering wood, and Stanton saw Ida talking with a man in the distance. He recognized Ida because she wasn't wearing a mop cap or pinner, and her blond hair gleamed in the sun. The man wore a wig, but Stanton couldn't see who he was. Could it be Cecil? He looked at Ralph and saw he'd noticed them too.

"I'll be right back," Ralph said as he headed for the couple.

The man must have seen Ralph striding their way, for he turned and vanished into the woods. Ida met Ralph, and they stood talking. Stanton couldn't tell if they argued or not, although he watched intently. In several minutes, Ralph came back to help unload the wood.

"She said the man came to see her about some prior business arrangement they'd had. She said she'd explain everything to me later, when we had more time to talk. It seems to be a lengthy tale."

"Tell me if there's something I should know or if you need my help," Stanton told him, and Ralph nodded. The worried but determined look on Ralph's face let Stanton know that he intended to get to the bottom of it.

"I don't think it's much to be concerned over," Ralph told him later when Stanton asked about Ida and the stranger. "I'll let you know if I learn any differently."

The gossipmongers seemed determined to smear Stanton's reputation. As soon as word got out about Ralph and Ida's upcoming wedding, the rumor spread that Ida was with child, Stanton was the father, and Ralph had been pressured into marrying her.

Beth deemed the gossip as ridiculous, and Stanton thanked God that she trusted him. If the rumors had been about her and Cecil, he didn't know if he'd have been as unconcerned.

Now that Stanton and Beth had been married for six months, he'd hoped Beth would be with child by now, and he would soon have a son, but it hadn't happened. Nothing lacked in their lovemaking, so perhaps the day would arrive soon. As long as he had Beth, he could wait. He knew she wanted children as much as he did.

"Have things gotten better between you and Ida?" Stanton asked Beth.

Ida had stopped flirting with him, and she seemed besotted with Ralph, but he wanted to make sure Beth felt okay with everything. She still didn't laugh as freely as she once had.

"Things are much better. We may never be the best of friends, but she's treating me with much more respect, and we get along well enough."

"I'll be glad when she's married and staying in the cabin with Ralph. I miss us having the house to ourselves."

"So do I." She gave him a coquettish grin, and he felt better.

Clouds layered the sky on the morning of Ralph and Ida's wedding and threatened snow. Stanton prayed nothing would happen to delay the wedding. Ralph hitched up the wagon with a worried look at the sky.

Beth had helped Ida dress and get ready for the wedding upstairs in Ida's bedroom. They'd made over a dress from Beth's trunk, and she looked nice, but not as lovely as Beth. Beth had a beauty that shone no matter what she wore.

Stanton had just helped Beth from the wagon, and they'd started for the church, when Fiona Fletcher approached. "Hello, Beth."

"Fiona, I didn't know you were back in Middleville."

"Yes, I came back for Christmas and will most likely stay here for a while. I think I had stayed too long at my aunt's in Boston. What was it Benjamin Franklin wrote in *Poor Richard's Almanack*? 'Visits should be short, like a winter's day, Lest you are too troublesome, hasten away.' The time had come for me to hasten away."

"I'm sure your parents are pleased to have you home," Beth said.

"You two are looking good. I think marriage must agree with you."

"It does," Stanton said. "I've never been happier."

Fiona didn't seem to know what to say. "I guess I should be joining my parents inside. It's good to see you two again."

"We wish you well," Stanton replied.

"Something about her seems different," Beth told Stanton. "I hope she's matured some."

The service went well, and so did the wedding. In a matter of minutes after the ceremony started, the pastor introduced Mr. and Mistress McCarthy. Beth wanted to leave soon in order to put the final touches on the wedding dinner. Ralph and Ida would come in one of the other wagons.

As they went outside, Stanton saw the clouds had cleared and the sun shone brightly. It had turned out to be a lovely day. Then, he noticed Horace, and the man looked rather pensive.

"Horace, I didn't know you were here."

"I came for the wedding. I sort of feel responsible for Ida, and I'm not sure this wedding is for the best."

"You have no reason for concern. Ralph is decent enough, and they seem taken with each other. I think the marriage will work out well. Ida seems to need a man in her life."

"As you seem to need a woman, I guess."

Stanton felt Beth stiffen beside him. What did Ralph mean by that statement? Stanton needed Beth, not just any woman.

"Please come to the dinner I've prepared in honor of the couple," Beth said. "We'd love to have you."

Stanton moved his arm around Beth. She'd invited Horace, although the man seemed less than cordial today, and he appreciated her effort to do the right thing.

Horace's expression changed to a friendly smile. "Thank you. I may take you up on the invitation, but I need to see to some business first. If I don't make it, you'll know something detained me elsewhere."

"You're doing business on the Lord's Day?" Stanton asked before he thought.

Horace frowned. "I'm not finalizing anything, just talking. I'll take my leave now." He shook hands with Stanton, tipped his hat to Beth, and left.

"Is he always so gloomy or serious acting?" Beth asked as Stanton led her to the wagon.

"I'd never thought about it, but I guess he is. He's always been friendly, though."

"Did Molly have other brothers and sisters?"

"No, just Horace. When I met her, her father was still alive, but he died after we married. He seemed happy to welcome me to the family. I don't think Horace felt that way at first, but he came around after Molly and I married. He's been a good brother-in-law."

"Do you miss having an extended family?"

"I liked your father very much, but I don't feel as if I'm missing anything. You're enough for me, Beth. We'll just start our own family."

She smiled. "I'm looking forward to that. You'll make a wonderful father."

Stanton's heart did a jig. This woman was perfect for him, and she would make an exceptional mother too.

The dinner went well. Agatha Denny helped Beth so Ida wouldn't need to. Everyone enjoyed the food, and the conversation never faltered.

Horace did come, but he didn't say much. He appeared uncomfortable and seemed to mainly watch Ida and Ralph or Beth. Stanton hoped Horace didn't become another one of Beth's admirers. He'd just been able to take Ralph off that list, and he had no desire to add another. Now, if he could just remove Cecil.

Before the guests began departing, Stanton noticed Horace standing with Ida outside by the corner of the house, telling her something. Ida seemed none too pleased, and when she came in, she looked pale.

What was going on? And why would Horace upset Ida on her wedding day?

Chapter Nineteen: Secrets

"An open foe may prove a curse but a pretended friend is worse."

—Poor Richard's Almanack

As Stanton had hoped, things became easier for Beth and him after the wedding. Ida moved her things into the cabin with Ralph, and the house became all theirs once more.

Ida came over on Fridays to dust and clean. On Monday Beth took her the laundry that needed washing, and Ida washed and ironed them at the cabin.

Stanton allowed Ralph and Ida to get the supplies they needed to cook, but he got to eat what Beth cooked, while Ralph had to eat Ida's cooking. It made sense to combine the cooking and meals, but Stanton didn't want that. He wanted Beth to himself.

Although their rapport had improved with Ida's absence, something seemed to be bothering Beth. At first he thought she might be expecting a baby, but that proved wrong. At last, he decided to ask her.

"Is something troubling you?" he asked one morning as they lay in bed, reluctant to move from the warm covers.

"Why have you never told me you love me?"

Stanton froze. Of all the things, he would have never expected this.

"Haven't I treated you well? Haven't I shown you how much I care for you?"

"You have, but you've never said you loved me. Isn't that normal for husbands and wives with a closeness like ours?"

"When we were courting and you listed the qualities you looked for in a husband, you didn't say anything about him loving you. You said you wanted an honest man who'd treat you well and be a close friend, the kind of man you can love and respect, and a man you could share everything with. I think I've been all those things to you. You never said anything about a man who would love you."

"Then you don't love me?" Her voice almost broke before she got the question out, and Stanton's throat tightened.

"Beth, I care for you more than I've ever cared for anyone in my life, but when my father killed himself because he couldn't live without my mother, I vowed never to love someone like that. Please understand. This has nothing to do with you and everything to do with me."

"You didn't love Molly either, then?"

"No. I didn't know how good a marriage could be until I married you. Molly and I got along well, but I realize now how shallow our marriage ran. It had none of the depth or closeness you and I share. I'm happy with you as my wife, Beth. Can't you be happy with me, even if I don't say I love you?"

"You're rejecting the greatest gift God has to offer. God loved us so much that he sent His Son to die for us. He gave us the capacity to love Him and to love each other. The love shared between a husband and wife is so special. By refusing to love, you're cheating yourself, cheating me, and cheating God. I do love you, Stanton, and I'm not afraid to say it."

Stanton lay stunned. Just when things had become easier for them again, this had to come up. Why was Beth making so much out of him saying he loved her? He cared for her, respected her, took good care of her, and held a great fondness for her, so what if he didn't love her? She seemed to hold some schoolgirl fantasy about love. Love caused more problems than it ever settled.

They got up and went about their day, but Stanton could sense the disagreement hanging between them. Neither spoke of it again, but he could tell neither forgot about it either. He could see it in her eyes, when she looked at him. He knew his refusal to love had hurt Beth, and he hated that, but he didn't know what to do about it. Saying he loved her wouldn't make it true, and he didn't want to lie to her, but he felt her disappointment in him, and it pierced his heart.

When they went to bed that night, Beth turned her back to him. For the first time in their marriage, she didn't come to lie in his arms.

"Beth, are you angry at me?" he asked as he put his hand on her upper arm.

"I'm not angry, just hurt."

"Why are you turning your back on me, then?"

"I just need some time to think through everything you said this morning. I'm confused and disillusioned."

He wanted to ask if she still loved him, but he understood the paradox of that. He wanted to comfort her and take away the pain he'd caused, but he didn't know how.

"I'll give you the time you need to sort things out, but please don't pull away from me. I need you, Beth. Don't make our lives more difficult. We're supposed to be as one."

He lifted up, swept her hair out of the way, and kissed her cheek. He guessed that would be the only kiss he would have tonight. He lay back down, but he knew sleep would be a long time coming. Even the bed felt cold and unwelcoming without Beth cuddled close to him.

Beth curled into a ball with her back to Stanton. Tears streamed down her face, but she did her best not to sob or sniff, so he wouldn't know. It seemed all her dreams had crumpled into nothing. Stanton would never love her. How would she cope?

She had never considered that they might have a loveless marriage, at least on Stanton's part. Stanton had always been so considerate and warm that she'd never guessed he refused to love anyone.

Dear Lord, please show me what to do now. I'm shocked and devastated by what Stanton told me, but I love him and want our marriage to be strong. Since I don't understand and don't know what to do, I put the situation in Thy hands. Take our lives and make them what Thou intended for them to be. I pray in Jesus's name. Amen.

Beth felt so alone, almost abandoned. Without Stanton, she had no one she could turn to except God. God would be enough. He would always be enough, but she wanted her husband too. She wanted the marriage they'd had at the beginning. Ida had stolen much of their bliss, and now Stanton's determination never to love drained her joy. Why did life have to be sprinkled with so much sorrow and heartache?

"But wait on the Lord, and He shall save thee. The Lord is good unto them that wait for Him, to the soul that seeketh Him."

She could wait. She'd cultivated patience after she fell and broke her leg and after her father's accident. She would wait upon the Lord. He would either take matters into His own hands or direct her path so she'd do the right thing.

Perhaps she'd put too much emphasis on Stanton recognizing and saying he loved her. He treated her with love, and actions mattered a great deal more than words. Could it be that he loved her now but refused to recognize or voice the sentiment, even to himself?

His father had committed suicide after his wife died, when Stanton had been but a boy. Because of his father's moment of weakness, Stanton blamed the love his father had for his mother and became determined to never love. But love could not be ordered about. Love could come unbidden and unaware. The more she thought about it, the more she decided Stanton might love her after all. At least, she could cling to that thought and have some hope.

Her tears had dried up after her prayer, so she turned over and moved closer to Stanton. Half the night had already passed, but she could tell by his breathing he hadn't gone to sleep either.

He slipped his arm under her neck and pulled her closer so her head rested on his shoulder. She reached up to kiss his cheek, as he had hers earlier, and she tasted the salty dampness. He'd been crying too, and that fact cut at her heart. If he didn't love her, then he cared a vast amount for her.

"Thank you, darling," he whispered.

"For what?"

"For coming back to me. For having an understanding heart."

She wanted to tell him that love did that and to say she loved him, but she thought it better not to use the word now. Instead, she moved her mouth to his.

The strained relationship between Stanton and Beth had eased somewhat and for that he rejoiced. They hadn't discussed the question of love again, but he knew it still lay between them, like a thick stone wall. However, Beth had seemed to have come to some decision in his favor, and her smiles and laughter brightened their home.

The late December clouds hung heavy and dark, threatening snow at any moment. The wind had picked up with a cutting cold, and Stanton was glad to be headed home. He guided a horse pulling a sled full of wood from the forest, and Ralph followed with another one.

Something troubled Ralph. Stanton had never seen the man so burdened, but it didn't seem to be a disagreement between him and Ida. They seemed to be close and sharing whatever problems confronted them.

Well, better a problem with Ralph than one with Beth. If he could make Beth's life easy, smooth, happy, and free of trouble, he would. He had begun to wonder if any person could do that for another, however. No matter how much he wanted or how hard he tried, troubles had kept coming up over the last months, like irksome weeds after a soaking rain. At least there'd still been no other attempts on anyone's life, and Ida and Ralph had seemed happy, until recently. Perhaps only God governed attributes like happiness. Yet despite the problems that came, Stanton knew God had blessed him well when he'd married Beth.

Thank you, Lord.

"Could I come over and talk with you after dinner?" Ralph asked him the following Sunday after Stanton and Beth had returned from church. Despite their invitation, Ralph and Ida chose not to attend the service.

"Of course," Stanton told him.

The request puzzled Stanton, but it made him curious to hear what Ralph had to say. His servant wouldn't have asked for the meeting if it hadn't been important.

After the meal, Ralph came into the house by himself, and the three of them sat in the parlor.

Ralph looked worried as he faced Stanton. "Ida has confided in me that she was sent here to cause problems. Someone told her to make Mistress Klein jealous, seduce you if she could, and do any damage possible. She picked the mushrooms thinking they might make you and Beth sick for a while. She swears she didn't know they could have killed you."

Beth gasped. "Why isn't Ida here?"

"She couldn't bear to face you. It took me a bit of talking to convince her you needed to know."

"Who did this?" Stanton asked, as he tried to subdue his rising anger.

"She refuses to tell. She says the man will kill her if she does. That's why she didn't want to tell me or you about it, because she thinks he'll kill anyone who knows."

"Is the man the same person who left the chicken heads, shot you and Beth, and set fire to the wheat?"

"Ida doesn't know, but I think that makes sense, don't you?"

"Let me go talk to Ida."

Beth followed the two men as they walked to the cabin. The afternoon sun looked warm and inviting, but it didn't feel that way. Beth wrapped her cloak closer around her. Thankfully, only a short walk brought them to the cabin. Ralph opened the door and let them in.

Ida wouldn't look at them. She wrung her hands and almost shook with fear.

"Ida, you've got to tell us who's behind this. We've got to put a stop to it."

She gave Stanton no answer, only stared down at the floor. Her hands twisted at her apron.

"If you don't tell me who it is, I'll let the sheriff take over. He'll get an answer from you, or you'll go to trial for attempted murder because of the mushrooms."

"You'll tell the sheriff anyway," she said quietly.

"That may be true, but it'll go easier for you if you cooperate, and I don't have to mention the mushrooms either."

"You need to tell them, darling." Ralph put his arm around her.

"It's Horace Sneed, isn't it?" Beth asked her in a soft voice. She had been sitting quietly observing.

Ida hesitated and then nodded. Stanton heard the question and saw Ida agree, but his mind wouldn't accept it. Molly and Horace had been close, but his brother-in-law had grown to like Stanton. They'd been friends, and Stanton couldn't believe he'd do such dastardly things.

"Why?" Stanton couldn't get much more out. Trying to process all this had rendered him almost speechless.

"He threatened to harm me if I didn't, and he promised to buy back my indenture, free me, give me a nice sum of money, and see I had a good position if I did." She barely looked up, but her entire countenance showed her shame and remorse.

Stanton stood. "I'll ride in to inform the sheriff. Beth, do you want to go with me?"

"Yes, I'd prefer to be near you."

"Ralph, keep the rifle with you and stay close to Ida, until an arrest is made."

"Do you think they'll take Ida's word over Mr. Sneed's?" Ralph asked.

"I think so, and now that we know where to look, there may be other evidence."

"I'm so sorry," Ida mumbled. She looked up for the first time and tears streamed down her face. "I'm so very sorry."

On the way to town, Beth sat close to Stanton in the wagon and wrapped blankets close around them. Stanton had tucked two warmers filled with hot coals near their feet.

She put a hand on his thigh in support, and he held the reins in one hand to grasp hers in the other.

"Why would Horace have turned on me like this?"

"I don't know. I don't think there's a good answer why anyone chooses sin over God's best for us. Maybe he felt you betrayed Molly when you married me, because that's when the incidents started."

"That doesn't make sense. If I had died first, I think Horace would have expected her to remarry."

"It doesn't make sense, but I don't think any of this does."

Chapter Twenty: Surprises

"Thy wife shall be as a fruitful vine by the sides of thine house: thy children like olive plants around thy table."

—Psalm 128:3

They found the sheriff right outside the jail, but he led them inside the small building. He appeared about as puzzled as Stanton over the information, but he said he would begin to investigate right away. He didn't know if Horace had already gone back to Philadelphia or not.

"I've noticed him in the area often in the last few months," the sheriff said, "but he always seemed like a nice enough fellow. I'd never have picked him out for a criminal."

"It's hard for me to believe too. I'm still hoping Ida's information proves wrong, but she seemed to be telling the truth."

Several days later, the sheriff told Stanton that Horace Sneed had seemed to disappear. His housekeeper in Philadelphia hadn't seen him in a long time, and no one around town had observed him since the wedding. The sheriff had sent word to the surrounding towns to be on the lookout for the man, but nothing had turned up so far. Horace had won Ida's indenture in a card game just like he'd said, but the man who had lost the hand of cards couldn't add any new information.

What the sheriff told him made Stanton uneasy. He didn't trust his onetime friend and feared what the man might try next. He hoped Horace would be apprehended well before it came time to plant in the spring. This had gone on too long already.

At first he'd tried to tell himself there'd been some kind of mistake and Horace was innocent. It had been hard to believe the worst of his brother-in-law and friend. When Horace appeared to be in hiding, however, Stanton had to admit he looked guilty. If he hadn't done anything wrong, why would he remain so hard to find?

"Stanton," Beth said after church on Sunday, "Cecil asked to come by the house this afternoon. He wants to talk to me about Fiona. I told him he could come."

Stanton said the first thing that came to mind. "You should have consulted me first."

He knew it had been the wrong thing to say as soon as it left his lips. She stiffened in the wagon seat, and he could sense her tension.

"Am I not allowed to invite someone to our home, or is it just your home?"

He managed to hold back his frustration because her voice tone had been soft and gentle, despite the biting words.

"Of course it's your home, but do you think inviting Cecil is a good idea? By your own admission, he's a cad, and I've seen how he flirts with you."

"Cecil doesn't flirt with me as much as Ida once did with you. Besides, you'll be there, Stanton. I told him that you would need to be in on our meeting."

Stanton frowned. " Still, I'm not sure it's a good idea. Most of the time I'm around Cecil, I feel like thrashing him."

She looked amused, as if she was holding back a smile. Didn't she think him serious?

"You may ask him to leave at any time, if you think he's acting improper."

"Uhh. I guess it's okay then, but I still don't like it. I just don't like Cecil Shippen."

She did smile up at him then, and he realized she could manipulate him without even trying. When she smiled at him like that, he would give her anything.

"What time is he coming?" Stanton asked in resignation.

Cecil arrived at the appointed time, and, as if to prove Stanton wrong, played the role of the perfect gentleman. Even Stanton could find no fault in his demeanor. Beth showed him into the parlor and offered him some refreshment, but he declined.

"I've been thinking that maybe I should marry Fiona," Cecil said after they'd sat down.

"Why have you changed your mind?" Beth asked him.

"Well, if the baby is mine, he should have my name. I hear he looks like me, but Fiona and I have similar coloring, so it could be hard to tell."

"Do you have any reason to believe she'd been seeing other men?" Beth asked.

"No. I think the boy is most likely mine."

"Were you the one she ran out to meet behind her house the Sunday I went there for dinner?" Stanton asked. "I noticed her hurrying to meet someone in the woods as I rode away."

"She came to meet me. What do you think, Beth? Should I marry her?"

"If Fiona will have you now, I think you should, as long as you can give up the other women. It would be better to leave things as they are, if you can't be faithful to a wife."

He seemed surprised but then smiled. "Well, now, that's something to consider, isn't it? You've always understood me better than anyone else, Beth, which is remarkable, since we're so different."

"I agree with Beth," Stanton added, "and you need to settle down. If you continue in your roguish ways, there'll come a time when you're going to find yourself in even deeper trouble. Your son deserves better. Where is he, by the way?"

"She left him with her aunt in Philadelphia, but she says she misses him. I'm sure you're right and that I should make some changes. You know, I think Fiona has changed too. She seems more mature since she's returned, as if she's made up her mind to be a better person."

"Maybe it's time for you to grow up too," Beth told him.

Cecil sat back in his seat and grew rigid, but then he seemed to consider what Beth had said, and he nodded. "You're probably right."

It amazed Stanton that Beth talked so bluntly to Cecil. But it made him feel better, too.

Cecil thanked them both and took his leave. He had stayed only about thirty minutes.

"Now, that wasn't so bad, do you think?" Beth asked him with that impish grin.

"Not so bad at all, but I'm glad he didn't stay long. I'm ready for an afternoon nap." He raised his eyebrows, hoping she would know what he really meant. "What about you?"

Monday morning they awoke to a blizzard. It had snowed a couple of times earlier but nothing like this. The wind howled around the corners, like a pack of wolves begging to get in out of the cold.

Stanton and Beth snuggled down in their covers and delayed getting out of bed as long as possible. Stanton cherished these moments with Beth nestled on his shoulder and cuddled against him.

"Stay here until I get the fire stoked," he told her. "Then I'll come back and let you get me warm, until the kitchen heats up some."

Stanton had hoped the snow would abate some before he had to go to the barn, but it still came down at a steady pace in its diagonal path from the gusts of wind. He had just wrapped up to brave the elements, when Ralph came in with the milk.

"You seemed to be getting a later start than usual, and I thought you might appreciate some help."

"I am grateful and glad that I don't have to go out in this. Thank you."

Being snowed in with Beth gave Stanton a special feeling. The rest of the world seemed locked away, and he could believe they were the only two people in existence. He loved it.

The blizzard had subsided, but the snow still blanketed the ground when Christmas arrived. The two couples had dinner on Christmas Eve together, but they decided to spend that evening and Christmas Day in their separate houses.

Beth and Stanton had a Christmas tree because both had been familiar with the custom from some of their

German relatives. Instead of having two trees, one for each of them, however, they decided to only have one larger evergreen, and put the presents for both of them under it.

They had fun bundling up and roaming the farm in search of the right tree, getting some of the decorations Stanton's family had had from storage, and choosing the best candles Beth had made. They played like children as they decorated and sat beside the tree sipping hot spiced apple cider and singing Christmas carols.

Christmas morning they hurried from bed like children, ate breakfast, and opened presents. Stanton gave Beth a pen-and-ink set, a blank journal, and wooden writing box with a slanted top he'd made for her. She seemed to love them.

She gave him two shirts she'd made—one for Sunday and one for everyday use, and her father's gold engraved pocket watch. He felt honored and thrilled.

Because of Beth, Stanton had never enjoyed a Christmas more. He and Molly had just gone through the motions and did the expected, but with Beth, everything had deeper meaning.

They ate a scrumptious dinner, had the leftovers for supper, and went to bed early. Stanton still enjoyed their private times together as much now as he had when they were first married, and, even more remarkable, Beth seemed to as well. He breathed in a contented sigh.

"I have one more special Christmas present for you," she told him as she lay snuggled against him.

"You've given me more than enough already."

"I think you'll be eager for this one." She paused. "We're going to have a baby."

He lay stunned for several seconds. Had he heard her right? Could he be getting his son at last? He wrapped his arms more tightly around her and kissed her, as a multitude of emotions welled up.

"That's wonderful," he said with his heart overflowing. "I'm so happy. When do you think it will be? Do you need to see the doctor?"

"The best I can determine, it should arrive sometime in June, and, no, I don't need a doctor. I'd prefer to have the midwife come."

"Beth, you must take good care of yourself now. I don't want you to work as hard as you did in the fall. You should take it easy and rest. Let Ida do more of the work."

"The Indians around here believe it's better to stay active in order to have a healthy baby, and I tend to agree. I won't overdo, but I need to stay busy. If I start having any problems, I'll rest more, but I don't expect that to happen."

"Don't fight me on this, Beth. I want you to be careful. This is too critical. Our baby is too important; you are too important."

He pulled her close and kissed her again to stop her protest. One way or the other, he'd see that she didn't exhaust herself.

Near the end of January, Stanton and Beth attended Cecil and Fiona's wedding. Beth guessed Cecil had decided he should settle down and support his family. She hoped everything would work out well for them.

It was a beautiful wedding, one of the most extravagant ones Beth had ever attended. Fiona made a stunning bride, and Cecil looked handsome in his formal clothes, although no man could ever look as good as Stanton.

She turned to look at him and caught his eye. He smiled at her, and she wondered if thoughts of their wedding filled him too.

Because it would soon be hard to hide her growing middle, Beth realized this would be the last time she could come out in public. From now on she would be compelled to stay around the farm.

Spring came early, but sometimes it just teased, and there'd be another cold interlude after a warm spell. Beth had enjoyed the winter more than any she could remember. She hadn't had to worry about keeping enough firewood or food, and she'd had Stanton to keep her company. Her husband brought joy to her days, and she wished those idyllic times could continue. However, she knew that with spring fast approaching, her husband would have to be in the fields all of the daylight hours, with the exception of Sundays.

She needed to get her garden started soon, too. She had it all planned out, and she couldn't wait to get her hands in the soil.

She'd had no complications with her pregnancy. There'd been some mild morning sickness for a while, but she didn't mention it, and it had usually worn off by midmorning. Now, she felt fine, even early in the morning.

She smiled. She found it endearing how Stanton worried over her, and she felt even more cherished. Could one be cherished without being loved?

On an April afternoon, Stanton insisted on helping Beth plant the garden, although she assured him she could use the hoe and do the work herself. He did make the planting much easier, but she felt guilty for taking him away from the fields, when he had so much to do there. Knowing he wouldn't change his mind, however, she conceded and enjoyed his help and company.

Stanton and Ralph went to the fields early the next morning. Beth decided to gather the eggs, so she headed for the chicken coop. The chickens roamed freely during the day, but Stanton had built them a place to roost at night with nests for the hens to lay their eggs in. He said it helped keep the predators from getting to them.

She'd gathered all the eggs she could find in the nests and had just stepped out of the chicken coop, when someone grabbed her and pulled her behind it. The man had one hand over her mouth and held her so hard she panicked. This had to be Horace Sneed, for she knew of no other who might wish her harm. She struggled to get away, but he held her too firmly.

He pulled her into the woods, and her heart pounded so hard she thought it might burst.

She tried to pull some coherent thoughts together. How long would Stanton be in the fields, and would he know where to find her, even when he discovered her missing? She needed to calm down and think clearly. She'd never be able to overpower the man, so she needed to use her wits and try to outsmart him. As he dragged her on, she tried to dig her feet into the ground in order to leave a visible path. It made it rougher on her, but it also made it more difficult on Horace to move her.

Beth didn't know how far he dragged her, but it seemed like miles. He didn't handle her with care either but pulled her through briars, brush, and branches. At least, her skirts gave her legs some protection. When he had her well away from the farm, he stopped.

"I'm going to take my hand away from your mouth, but if you scream or call for help, I'll kill you." His voiced sounded cold and calloused. "I'd rather wait and make Stanton suffer and anguish over the fact I have you, but if I need to kill you sooner, I won't hesitate."

He dropped his hand, and Beth saw Horace looking at her belly. His eyes took on an evil gleam.

"Well, well. So you're carrying the man's brat. That's how he killed my Molly, you know. I'll see that yours never lives either."

Beth tried not to panic, but his words chilled her to the bone. She knew now would be the best time to do something, but running would be futile. She looked at him with a terror she didn't even have to feign.

"So, your bold ways are leaving you, are they? I like to see the fear in your face."

Beth collapsed to the ground and pretended to be unconscious. Let the man think she'd fainted. It might not give her an opportunity to escape, but she couldn't think of anything better right now.

"All right, woman. You stay right there, while I get the rope from my horse to bind you. I'm glad you passed out and made it easy for me, because I wondered how I would manage."

She heard him walk away, but from the sound of his footsteps in the leaves, he didn't go as far as she would have liked. She heard the horse whinny and stomp, and she eased up.

A quick glance showed the horse twisting away from him as he fought to gain control. The horse must not like him any better than she did.

She moved in the other direction and hoped the horse would keep him occupied until she was out of sight. At least, she didn't think he heard her departure over the noise he and the horse were making.

Once hidden among the trees, she moved faster, but the sound of the leaves crunching beneath her steps concerned her. She angled her path so she would come out at the farm and not run into Horace.

She heard his voice but couldn't tell what he'd said because of her movement and the distance. She guessed he'd discovered her missing and cursed her. She didn't dare look back, because she didn't want to slow for a second.

Chapter Twenty-One: The Downfall

"Ye have sinned against the Lord: and be sure your sin will find you out."

—Numbers 32:23

Beth could hear Horace coming, and she ducked behind a giant oak. She tried not to move a muscle for fear of giving him clues to her whereabouts. Leaning against the tree, she saw a squirrel in the tree next to her and prayed the little animal wouldn't give her away, but it moved off to her right, hopping from tree to tree near their tops. It then scampered to the ground, where the trees thinned. She hoped it wouldn't head back her way, but it ran in the opposite direction.

"I've got you now," she heard Horace yell as he took off after the sound of the squirrel. Beth had always been amazed by how much noise a small creature could make in the leaves, but now she thanked God for it.

She resumed walking in the other direction, trying hard to make as little noise as she could and hoping the squirrel continued to make more.

"Beth! Beth!" She heard Stanton's frantic cry, but she was afraid to answer him yet. Instead, she headed toward his voice as quickly and quietly as she could. She thought she heard footsteps behind her, but they didn't sound near, and she couldn't be sure.

"Stanton! I'm here!" She moved toward the sound of his voice.

"Beth! Is that you? Keep calling, so I can find you."

"Stanton!" she yelled. Then she saw him and ran into his arms.

"Oh, darling, what happened? I found the egg basket thrown on the ground, and my heart almost stopped."

"Horace is out there. He grabbed me and pulled me into the forest. By God's grace, I managed to escape, but please take me home."

"Are you all right? Did he hurt you?"

"There's only minor wounds where he held my mouth and dragged me through the woods. I'm scared but fine."

Before she had a chance to protest, Stanton scooped her up and carried her to the house. His arms comforted her, and she gladly snuggled against his chest. He had her lie down, and while he cleaned her scratches, she told him what had happened but left out the part about Horace saying Stanton had killed Molly by getting her with child. Beth didn't want him blaming himself more than he already did. She could see his jaws clench and the concern in his eyes as she told her story.

"I wanted to go after Horace," Stanton told her. "He needs to be stopped. But I knew you needed me to care for you, and I couldn't leave you."

"I'm glad you're here." She looked him in the eye to let him see the truth of her words. She praised God that he hadn't tried to apprehend that deranged man. She couldn't bear the thoughts of possibly losing Stanton.

Stanton sent Ralph to tell the sheriff what had happened and came back to sit with Beth. "I know Horace will likely be long gone before the sheriff gets here, but he should know. When I found where you dropped the eggs, I'd never been so frightened in my life. I was so afraid I'd lost you and the baby—like before."

His voice quivered, and Beth reached out and took his hand. "I'm still here. You haven't lost me or the baby."

He sat on the bed beside her and took her into his arms. He held as if she were made of eggshells and would crumble if he touched her, but she knew he had to reassure himself of her presence.

"I'm not going to break," she told him as she put her arms around him and squeezed.

As his arms tightened around her, she relaxed against him. The whole experience had left her as weak as pauper's tea.

Stanton had been right about Horace, because he'd disappeared again. Although the sheriff brought some men to help him, they didn't find him in the forest or surrounding area. Just to be sure, Stanton and Ralph made a thorough search of the barn and outbuildings, but no evidence turned up showing that Horace had ever been there.

Beth turned her fears over to God, but Stanton had more difficulty. She asked Stanton if they could begin having a nightly family devotion, since it would be good for their children, and he agreed. She read all the passages she could find in the Bible about trusting in the Lord. Stanton gave the readings his full attention, but he said little, and she didn't know if they helped him or not. She knew he still tried to do everything he could think of to protect her.

The sheriff didn't locate Horace as quickly as they'd hoped, and Beth knew Stanton worried. When the women had work they had to do at the house, one of the men stayed near with his rifle. When they could, she and Ida went to the fields, too, but Stanton wouldn't allow Beth to do much.

On Thursday afternoon, they'd just come from the fields when Beth heard a scream, but it stopped abruptly. She looked out. The men had been in the barn, and Ralph came running out with his gun in his hand. Stanton followed.

When the men didn't see anything, Ralph ran to his cabin and then came to see if Ida was in the house. . When they couldn't find her anywhere, Ralph took off for Middleville and the sheriff at a frantic pace.

Fear gripped Beth, and she turned to Stanton, who stood near her. He must have seen her fear, because he took her in his arms, and pulled her close.

"We need to believe that Ida will be all right, and worry won't help," he said softly. This may be the break the sheriff needs to capture Horace. We'll pray for that."

Beth nodded. She hoped Horace would stick to the road, and he would be apprehended without anyone getting hurt.

"Horace will probably head for wherever he's been hiding," Stanton told Beth. "I just wish we could figure out where that is."

Stanton refused to leave Beth's side for fear Horace might return for her. She prayed and tried to turn the situation over to God, but she could do little for thinking of it.

"My grandfather used to say that revenge is a dish best served cold and not hot." Stanton shook his head. "I think Horace has become obsessed with trying to avenge what he sees as wrong done to Molly."

Beth puzzled over the statement. "I'm not sure what that means. I'd say revenge is a dish that shouldn't be served at all."

Stanton nodded in agreement. "I just don't understand. How can someone I knew as a good man be so filled with hatred?"

"He's certainly not thinking straight," Beth said. "His actions have made little sense."

Ralph came back driving Agatha Denny's wagon with the horse he'd ridden tied behind. Mistress Denny sat beside him. Stanton went out to help the lady down.

"The sheriff said he felt it useless to come out here now," Ralph reported, "but he's going around to everyone in town and asking questions to see if anyone knows anything." His voice shook and he looked pale and sick.

"I told him to be sure to question Agnes Knotts," Mistress Denny said. "That woman's been acting strange lately, even for her."

"Come in Mistress Denny," Beth said. "I think we all could use some tea."

"You come too, Ralph," Stanton said. "I'm sure you could use something to drink."

"With Ida missing and you in the family way, Mistress Klein, I thought you could use some help," Mistress Denny said.

Beth looked at her. "I appreciate your thoughtfulness, but I'm sure we'll manage just fine."

"Let me finish cooking supper and see to the cleanup. I can at least do that much."

For a woman Mistress Denny's size, she managed to finish cooking the meal in record time. They tried to eat some for her benefit, but no one had much appetite.

After she washed the dishes and thoroughly cleaned the kitchen, she insisted she could drive herself home, and, no, she wasn't worried about Horace Sneed being about. She'd learned to handle a gun years ago and had one right under the wagon seat. She didn't need an escort, either, for the good Lord would keep her safe.

"If Ida doesn't turn up, I'll be back Monday to do the washing and help with anything else you need me for," she whispered to Beth, as she got ready to leave. "You don't need to be bending over scrubbing those dirty clothes in your condition. If you need anything before then, you just send for me."

"Plenty of women continue to do all their work while they're expecting a child," Beth told Stanton as Mistress Denny drove off.

"But you're my wife, and not plenty of women. I agree with Mistress Denny."

"I should have known you would." But how could she fault him for trying to be so careful with her?

None of them slept much that night. Beth napped a little, but she didn't think Stanton slept at all, and a light burned in the cabin every time she looked out.

Stanton felt sorry for Ralph. He could imagine how the servant felt, because he'd been so distraught when Beth had been taken. At least Beth had managed to escape, and Stanton hadn't had to endure days of wondering what had happened to her. He knew he would have never managed that!

Ralph went into Middleville early the next morning to see what progress the sheriff had made. Stanton thought about going with him, but he wouldn't leave Beth.

Ralph came back later in the day without anything new to report. Saturday they all tried to stay busy, although Stanton and Ralph stayed close to the house. Having something to do did seem to help channel some of Stanton's nervous energy, but he couldn't get his mind off Ida, Horace, and the threat that hung over them all, as long as Horace remained free.

Beth tried to get Stanton to go to church without her Sunday, but he hesitated. He wanted to be with her and tried to talk her into holding their own Bible study instead. She had grown too large now to go out in public.

Stanton didn't think she looked unsightly, nor did he consider her condition so obscene it should be hidden away, but Beth didn't seem to mind following the rule. He didn't know if she felt unattractive or if she didn't want to travel in the bumpy wagon in her condition.

With mixed feelings, he got dressed in his suit and left in the wagon. Ralph promised to guard Beth, and, at least, Stanton hoped to hear some news.

Since he'd come by himself, he decided to go to the Lutheran church this time. It had been a while since he'd heard Reverend Durk preach.

As he stood outside for a brief moment to greet some of the men, Widow Knotts came hurrying up to him. "Mr. Klein, could I have a word with you please."

Oh, no! He should have gone to the Presbyterian church to avoid this woman. He must not have been thinking. He started to refuse her, but the serious look on her face made him change his mind.

"Let's make this fast," he said as he walked away from the men.

She followed him to the corner of the church building and looked around, as if she feared someone might be watching. "Horace Sneed has Ida at my house."

Stanton froze. Had he heard her correctly or was his mind playing tricks on him? "W-what did you say?"

"Horace has been hiding out at my place. I convinced him people would become suspicious if I didn't attend church, and the preacher would be sure to call to see what was wrong. He's threatened both me and Ida. What should I do?"

"Go get the sheriff. I'll go to your house and keep an eye on things." He looked at her trying to determine if he could trust her to do this. "You be sure to get the sheriff now. I'm counting on you, and it could be bad for me or Ida if Horace discovers me. Besides, the sheriff is bound to be lenient on any part you may have played in this, if you're the one to turn Horace in."

She nodded. "I'll hurry." She took off at a fast pace.

Stanton got his horse and led him down the street. He tied him at a hitching post not directly in sight of the widow's house, and got his rifle. He eased around to the back of the house next door and looked around.

The widow had some high bushes planted in the back of her small lot, and Stanton made his way to those, being careful not to be seen. They would give him a good place to hide until the sheriff arrived.

He hadn't been hidden long, when he heard the back door open. He peered through the bushes just enough to see Horace heading for the outhouse.

Wishing he had the materials to lock him in, Stanton stood to the side, where he would be largely hidden by the opening door. He held his rifle ready.

When Horace exited the tiny structure, Stanton raised his rifle and used the end of the stock to come down on Horace's head. He crumbled to the ground.

Feeling for the fallen man's pulse, Stanton determined it remained strong. He wanted to go check on Ida, but he knew he needed to make sure Horace didn't get away. He wondered if he should try to find something to tie the man up with, when he heard the back door open and saw the sheriff walk out.

"Well, it looks as if you've made things easy for me," he told Stanton, as he secured Horace. "The Widow Knotts is inside with Ida. We found her tied up, but she seems unharmed."

Stanton nodded at Horace. "Are you going to take him to the jail now?"

"Yes. I brought a wagon. If you'll help me get him in it, we'll collect the women and go there now. I need to ask them some questions, and then you can take Ida home. I know Ralph needs to know she's okay."

When they arrived at the jail, they helped the women down, and Stanton helped the sheriff get Horace locked in the jail. He would have liked to stay and heard the questioning, but the sheriff asked him to wait in the wagon.

Stanton had tied his horse to the back and would borrow the wagon to take Ida back. The sheriff said he would ride out soon to get it.

In about fifteen minutes, the sheriff led Ida out. "I'll let you take her home. I'll likely be out tomorrow to collect my wagon and I'll fill you in more then."

"Are you doing all right?" Stanton asked Ida as they started off.

"I am now. Thank you for your part in rescuing me and capturing Horace."

"You're very welcome. I'm so glad it's over."

She nodded and grew quiet. Stanton decided she probably needed the time and didn't try to make conversation.

Beth and Ralph came flying out of the house before the wagon came to a complete stop. Ralph pulled Ida into his arms and held her, as if he'd never let go. She clung to him with tears streaming down her face.

"You're later than I expected," Beth told Stanton, "and I feared something had happened."

He took her in his arms and kissed her forehead. "Let's get inside and I'll tell you all about it."

"Ida and I are going to our cabin," Ralph said. He shook Stanton's hand and thanked him profusely. "We'll see you later."

The sheriff came out after breakfast the next morning. Ralph and Ida came over when they saw him, and they all sat down to a cup of tea. Then the sheriff began to give them the gist of what he'd learned. "Widow Knotts said she'd been helping Sneed, because she knew he had a grudge against Stanton, and she did too, but she didn't know all Sneed's misdeeds. When he brought Ida to her house, she became upset, but by this time she'd grown to fear Sneed. After I questioned her the first time, she became distraught. She told Sneed that people would become suspicious if she didn't go to church, and she decided to talk to Stanton when she saw him there."

"Mr. Sneed didn't harm me, because he planned to get Ralph to kidnap Mistress Klein and swap her for me. He knew Ralph could get close to her, and Mr. Klein had been protecting her too much for him to capture her again. Mistress Knotts had him delay his plans of contacting you, until things settled down some."

"Some of you may need to testify at Sneed's trial," the sheriff said.

"What will happen to Widow Knotts?" Beth asked.

"She claims she didn't know what Sneed had been doing until he brought Ida there, and then she'd been too scared of him to do much. She said that as soon as she had a chance, she told someone. ."

"Why didn't she just tell you when you questioned her?" Ralph asked.

"She said Sneed would have harmed Ida then. There's not much evidence that she did anything criminally wrong. It wasn't wise to let Sneed stay at her place, but I'm not sure we could even prove immorality. I imagine she'll be moving soon, however, because her reputation's ruined here."

"Did Horace say why he'd done all this?" Stanton asked the sheriff.

"Seems he has some fool notion that you took Molly away from him. He says he should have kept her in Philadelphia, and he didn't because Molly and their father wanted her to marry you. He believes that if she'd have stayed with him, she'd still be alive today. He's not making much sense, if you ask me, because he seems to blame you for Molly's death."

After the sheriff left, the two couples ate dinner together and celebrated both Ida's return and Horace's capture. Stanton told Ralph and Ida to take the rest of the day and the following day off and spend the time together.

Stanton hadn't realized how worried he'd been. Now with Horace no longer a threat, he felt as if he'd been set free of weighty bonds. He and Beth said a special prayer of thanks that night.

Chapter Twenty-Two: The Realization

"Unto the woman he said, I will greatly multiply thy sorrow and thy conception; in sorrow thou shalt bring forth children; and thy desire shall be in thy husband."

—Genesis 3:16

A week later, news came that Horace Sneed had been shot trying to escape. He still breathed, but, according to the doctor, death hovered near.

Stanton felt a great sense of sadness. The man had made poor decisions and thrown his life away. He'd let his obsession rule his life. What a shame!

Both pastors went to speak with Horace before he died. Stanton didn't ask if he'd repented, but he prayed he did. He didn't attend the funeral either, because Beth couldn't go with him.

June came, but the baby didn't. Beth didn't seem worried, because she said she couldn't be sure of the time, but she seemed big enough for it to come soon. Stanton tried not to worry, but he did anyway. He didn't want to leave Beth to do his outside work, but he didn't have much choice. He had Ida stay in the house when he couldn't.

The midwife had come, made her initial examination, and told them everything looked fine. She said to send for her when the time came, but not to worry. The first one often came slowly.

As the days came and went, both Stanton and Beth became eager for the baby to come, but Stanton also dreaded the day. He prayed for a healthy son and for Beth to be all right. He felt a little guilty for wanting a boy so badly, but it didn't change how he felt. He hoped God understood.

Stanton remembered what had happened with Molly, and fear took hold. He tried to put in all in God's hands, as Beth had tried to show him, but he never succeeded for long. He both wanted it to be over and dreaded it coming, because he knew something could go wrong. How well he knew!

Beth became so uncomfortable she wanted the birth over with as soon as possible. She'd become larger than either one of them had expected, and the hotter summer weather added to her misery. Molly, even with her heavier figure, had not protruded as much as Beth did. Stanton worried the baby might be growing too large.

Stanton woke up as soon as he felt Beth get out of bed. "Is something wrong?" he asked when he realized she hadn't pulled out the chamber pot.

"It's hard for me to get comfortable," she told him. "Go back to sleep. I just need be up for a while."

"If you're getting up, then I'm getting up with you." He got up and put on his pants.

"I know better than to try to change your mind. You've been quite stubborn, since I told you about the baby."

"I just want to take the best possible care of you."

"You do that. You do it very well." She smiled at him then, and he felt better.

Beth sat in the chair and opened her Bible, but in a few minutes she closed it. She got up and began walking around the room.

"Can't read?" Stanton asked.

"No, I feel restless."

By dawn, she couldn't hide her discomfort. Stanton felt his pulse quicken.

"Is it time? Do I need to fetch the midwife?"

"I think so," Beth said as she sat down on the edge of the bed in apparent pain.

Stanton ran, got Ralph to ride for the midwife, and rushed back to Beth. Ida had offered to sit with her, but he declined. He wanted to stay with his wife now, because he knew the midwife would soon run him out.

When he returned, he found Beth had gone back to bed. He sat beside her and took her hand.

"You look so worried," she said, as she used her hand to wipe some of the frown lines on his forehead. "Trust in God, Stanton. Trust Him completely that whatever happens is for the best. Trust Him to take care of me. I do, and you should know that, whatever happens, He'll be with us. Take comfort in that."

Comfort! He had no comfort right now, and what Beth said didn't make him feel a bit better. She spoke as if she expected something bad to happen.

God, please don't let anything bad happen to Beth or my child. Please keep them from all harm. Have mercy on us. I've lost one wife and child, and I don't know what I'll do if I lose another. Lord, You know how hard it would be on me to have to bury Beth. Please, please be merciful toward us.

"Trust in the Lord with all thine heart; and lean not unto thine own understanding."

Where had that come from? Beth had read or quoted that verse from Proverbs several times, but now it sounded in his head, as if someone had spoken it.

He heard Ralph's horse outside, and he knew the midwife would soon be here. He gently pulled Beth into his arms and kissed her.

"Mistress Ebert is going to run me out now," he whispered in Beth's ear as he laid her back down.

"I love you, Stanton," Beth whispered to him.

Stanton could tell she was trying to put on a brave front. "Beth, I…"

"Mr. Klein, you need to leave the room so I can examine your wife and see how far along we are."

He nodded but kissed Beth's hand before he left. He stood outside the closed chamber door for a while, closed his eyes, and prayed again.

Beth had told him she loved him for only the second time. He had wanted to hear those words from her lips many times, but how could he expect her to say them when he couldn't?

"Things look fine," he heard the midwife tell Beth. "From the look of things, you should have a baby in a few hours."

Stanton breathed a sigh of relief at the first part of the report, but why did childbearing take so long? Would he be able to bear several hours of an agonizing wait? He'd have to, and, if Beth could endure that long with the pain, he shouldn't complain about waiting.

"I'm going to the kitchen to make some preparations," Mistress Ebert told him as she came out the door. "You can go in and sit with her until I get back, if you'd like. Don't be surprised if she has some pains hit her, but they're not coming close together, and nothing's going to happen yet."

The woman surprised him. He hadn't expected this, but it pleased him.

He sat in a chair pulled close to the bed and held Beth's hand. She would grip his now and then, when a pain came. The strength he felt in her grasp encouraged him.

He noticed the sweat on her brow and got a cloth, wet it in the basin, and wiped her forehead. She smiled up at him.

"Thank you, darling."

"Well, now," Mistress Ebert said as she entered the room carrying a pitcher of drinking water and some cloths with her, "you seem to be a right handy man to have around."

"He is indeed," Beth said.

"Sorry, but I need you to leave again, although, if you'd stay in the house for now, I'll call you to bring up the water I have heating after a while."

As the time ticked by, Stanton found he couldn't sit still. He spent much of the time pacing or walking up the stairs to stand at the door to see if he could tell what was going on.

Ida came over to see about dinner, but Stanton didn't want anything to eat. She told him to call her if she was needed, or when the baby came. She took the midwife a bowl of stew and some bread she'd brought over from the cabin.

The midwife called for the heated water just before suppertime. Stanton carried it up, and the woman took it from him at the door. He got a peek at Beth, and she looked much too haggard to suit him. Surely it wouldn't take much longer.

When Beth started groaning and crying out, Stanton nearly lost his mind. He would have rushed up those stairs if he hadn't thought he'd get in the way and complicate matters. Mrs. Ebert would be bound to run him out anyway.

About thirty minutes later by the clock, although it seemed more like days, Stanton heard a baby's tiny cry. He jerked to attention. That had to be a good sign, didn't it?

The midwife poked her head out the door. "You've got a son, Mr. Klein, but wait there until I get him and his mother cleaned up. If you want to do something, go get Ida to take care of the soiled linens."

A son! God be praised, he had his son.

"Is Beth okay?" he managed to ask before she closed the door.

"She came through fine, and should recover without a problem. The baby's on the small side, but he seems to be healthy."

Stanton got Ida and sent her up, but his summons didn't come. How long did it take to clean them up? If he didn't hear something soon, he would barge through the door regardless.

At last, Ida came out, but instead of carrying the linens, she held the baby. She also looked worried.

"I'm going to have Ralph ride for the doctor," she said. The midwife doesn't know what's happening, but Beth is still in pain, and after the baby came, things never finished as they should. Mistress Ebert asks that you hold the baby."

Stanton took the baby. He could see him now, despite how bundled they had him. He seemed awfully small, but he looked healthy otherwise.

Stanton had to sit down for fear he'd drop the baby she handed him. He'd grown too weak to stand. *God, please don't let anything happen to Beth.*

His whole body had become as helpless as a baby bird blown from its nest in a windstorm. He looked down at the small bundle in his arms. The infant moved his tiny arms, as if he were fighting against his new surroundings.

"It's okay, little fellow," he told the baby. "The worst is over now, and everything will be just fine."

But would it be? He felt his heart being pulled from his chest.

Don't go to pieces yet, he told himself. *Beth might need you, and you should wait and hear what the doctor has to say.*

His son started crying, and Stanton sucked in a deep breath, stood, and walked around with him. He hummed softly, and the baby quieted. The boy already proved to be a blessing, for he prevented Stanton from sinking too far into despair.

He didn't know how many steps he'd walked across the floor before the doctor came. It felt like miles. Mistress Ebert hadn't come from the room at all.

"Please let me know how Beth's doing and what's happening," Stanton told him as he came through the front door.

The doctor stood nearly as tall as Stanton but had white hair and piercing blue eyes. He exuded confidence, and Stanton felt better that he'd come.

"I'll probably send Mistress Ebert down with the report." He moved the swaddling and looked at the baby. "You have a good looking son here, Mr. Klein. Don't be surprised if he cries and won't hush, though. He's going to be very hungry. Let me go see if we can get his mother fixed up, so she can feed him."

Mistress Ebert came down wringing her hands. "I thought your wife had some sort of blockage keeping the afterbirth from coming, but the doctor has examined her and says it's another baby. This one is not turned right, and we're going to try to move it around." Her face showed her worry.

Stanton felt gripped by a fear that threatened to devour him. "H-h-how is Beth doing?"

She's exhausted and in a lot of pain. She's trying her best, but I just hope she doesn't grow too weak to do the pushing we need. This is the most complicated birthing I've ever seen." She shook her head.

Stanton had to sit down again. He almost felt numb from the pain he felt. He heard the baby crying in his arms, but he just sat and stared. It felt as if his body had shut down. He couldn't even think.

Ida came in to check on things and see if he wanted some supper. He didn't, but he sent the baby with her to her cabin. It shouldn't be left in his care the way he felt now. He knew Ida thought the baby's crying was upsetting Stanton more, but his thoughts were all on Beth.

What would he do if he lost Beth? He couldn't even begin to imagine how he would handle that. Even his son wouldn't be enough to replace her.

He jerked as if he'd been shot. A sudden understanding fell upon him like a giant boulder. This had been how his father had felt. He sat back and let the new revelation work itself around.

What a fool Stanton had been! He'd fallen in love with Beth even before he married her. He'd just refused to admit it. No, that wasn't correct. Love wasn't about falling. It went better with soaring, gliding, and climbing to new heights.

He'd loved her with every particle within him, but he'd called it fondness, caring, deep regard, and anything, except what it was—love. What had Shakespeare said? "A rose by any other name would smell as sweet."

Lord, please, please give me a chance to tell Beth how much I love her. She has complete trust in Thee. Don't let her die.

"Trust in the Lord with all thine heart; and lean not unto thine own understanding." That voice had returned again.

Complete trust. How did one go about getting it? If he could turn everything over to God, would Beth get better? Could he turn everything over to God?

His whole motivation in marrying again had been to have a son. Now he had his son, and it meant nothing without Beth. What a paradox! How stupid he'd been!

Love. What had been some of the things Beth had tried to tell him? Love came from God, and only God had perfect love. He should accept God's love and love Him back. The Bible listed loving God with all your heart as the most important commandment of all. The second told him to love others. If he loved God with all his heart, then that love would spill over into others. Loving God might even perfect his love for Beth and for his son. He knew he was far from perfect in any area of his life apart from Christ.

God, I want to follow Thy commandments, but You know how weak I am. I fight for my own way. Please take my life and do with it as You wish. Make me into the person You want me to be. As your Son prayed, not my will but Thine be done. Teach me to love Thee first and foremost, and give me the opportunity to tell and show Beth how much I love her. Grant that she can stay with me and help me rear our son, but help me to submit to whatever Thy will is. I pray, in Jesus' holy name. Amen.

He seemed to be able to think a little clearer after he prayed. He wasn't about to sit down and wait. Mistress

Ebert should have given him more information by now. He'd just go up and see for himself.

He looked at his pocket watch as he climbed the stairs. The doctor had been here for three hours.

He had gotten to the top of the steps, when he heard the weak cry of a baby. He'd forgotten to pray for this baby too. He'd been too concerned about Beth. He stopped and bowed his head and prayed for it, as well as for Beth again, before he opened the door.

"You have another son," the doctor said as he pushed Stanton out of the room, "and, although your wife has had a rough time, she's still with us. Go get Ida to help clean up, and I'll let you see her when you get back."

Stanton was relieved that Beth was alive, but the doctor's encouragement had sounded falsified and forced. The fact that she'd made it so far didn't mean she would continue to do so. He put his head against the wall in despair. He could tell by the doctor's tone of voice she might not make it. He gasped for air, turned, and propped himself against the wall. When he felt he could walk, he remembered his task at hand.

Stanton hurried to get Ida so he could see his wife for himself. Ida carried a squalling baby back with her. Stanton ran up the stairs first, with Ida coming behind. He shoved the door open and rushed in.

Beth looked horrible. The color had left her, and her eyes were closed. Her breathing seemed shallow; her chest barely moved. Stanton stood immobile beside the bed and stared at her.

Chapter Twenty-Three: Twins

"Notwithstanding, she shall be saved in childbearing, if they continue in faith and charity and holiness with sobriety."

—1 Timothy 2:15

"See if you can rouse her," the doctor said. "We need to have her feed your first son."

"Beth, wake up." She looked so tired Stanton hated to disturb her. "Wake up and see our two sons. We have twin boys, Beth."

She didn't stir, and Stanton looked to the doctor in concern. Ida grabbed the soiled linens and left the room with tears in her eyes. Stanton looked back at Beth, afraid she'd stopped breathing.

Mistress Ebert seemed calm as she handed Stanton a damp cloth, and he washed Beth's face with all the tenderness he felt for her. When he saw her eyelids move but not open, he leaned down and kissed her cheek.

"I love you, Beth," he whispered. "Do you hear me? I love you so much. Don't you dare leave me and our two boys. We need you. I don't think I can live without you."

Her eyes opened then. "You mustn't be like your father." Her soft voice quivered, and he had to strain to hear her. "No matter what happens, you must be here for our boys."

The doctor stopped packing his bag and said, "What are you two talking about? Mistress Klein needs to conserve her energy."

"The doctor's right, Beth. We'll talk more when you're stronger. Right now you have to regain your strength, because you have three people depending on you."

"Okay, now, Mistress Klein," Mistress Ebert said, "Let's prop you up some, so you can feed your firstborn son. He seems to think he's about to starve."

While Mistress Ebert helped Beth, Stanton went to look at the last twin. He'd been so concerned about Beth he hadn't even seen this boy yet. The baby looked to be a smaller replica of his brother, but he slept.

The baby Beth fed must have gotten satisfied, because he quit crying and fell asleep once he'd finished. The two babies both lay at opposite ends in the same cradle, and they were so small their feet didn't touch.

"Let's get out of here and let her rest," the doctor announced. "When you hear the smaller twin crying, he'll need to be fed. Give your wife as much to eat or drink as you can. Broth will be good to start with. Keep her in bed for a least a week. She lost a lot of blood, and I want her to get plenty of rest. Alternate the feeding of the twins as much as you can, but don't feed any one of them more often than two hours apart."

"The doctor is going to see me home," Mistress Ebert said. "I'll come by and see her tomorrow afternoon, and the doctor will be by later in the week. Let Ida take over here."

Stanton paid them both, walked them out, and tiptoed upstairs. He needn't have bothered being quiet, because all three of them were sound asleep. He stood and watched his sleeping sons. He could scarce believe these little ones were his sons. What a miracle!

He knelt down beside Beth's bed, thanked God she remained with him, and asked God to continue to heal her. He sat in the chair beside her and laid his hand over one of hers. He just needed to touch and be near her.

He checked on the twins, but neither stirred, so he went downstairs, ate a quick bite of stew Ida had left, and dipped up some of the broth into a cup for Beth. The smaller twin had begun to cry when he got back to their chamber.

He considered going after Ida, but he decided he could help as well as she could. He picked up the crying baby and marveled at how tiny and light he felt. When he put it on the bed beside Beth, she woke up. She still seemed exhausted. He elevated her head with pillows and put the baby in her arms. With a little encouragement, he began to feed.

"We need to name them," Beth said in a weak voice. "Is there someone you'd like to name them after?"

"Not really. Let's give them new names, all their own."

"Okay, what do you think about Michael and Gabriel, from the angels in the Bible? Don't you think they look like little angels?"

"Michael and Gabriel Klein." Stanton let the names play on his lips. "I like that. I guess Michael will be the firstborn and Gabriel the second. Michael is about three hours older than Gabriel."

"Is that right? I lost all track of time."

Stanton put Gabriel back in the cradle and helped Beth drink her broth. She managed a little over half the cup before she tired and needed to lie back down. He sat down in the chair beside her and read his Bible.

When Michael woke up, he had wet his clothing, so Stanton changed the linens. He didn't know what he was doing, but Beth had wanted to keep her babies clean, so he did his best.

What had his grandmother said? God sent children because of what they would teach their parents, as well as for what their parents would teach them. He had a feeling his lessons had begun.

Beth woke up when she heard Michael cry. Stanton noticed he had more lung power than Gabriel. He thought Beth's color looked a little better, but he might have been seeing what he wanted to see. Still, Stanton took hope that she seemed to be recovering some. After the baby finished, she drank some cider and lay back down.

"Shall I get Ida to spend the night with you and hand you the babies when they need feeding? The doctor said you were not to get out of bed."

"I would rest better if you were beside me." She patted his usual place in the bed. "However, I'll understand if you don't want the bother. You're not apt to get much sleep."

"How could my wife and children ever be a bother? I feel so blessed, Beth, but are you sure I won't bother you? I want you to get your rest."

"I'm sure. I would never think you're a bother."

He undressed and eased down beside her. She reached over and placed her hand in his. He would have loved to have her lay in his arms, but he didn't want to move her too much, in case she might start bleeding too much again.

Beth had been right. He didn't get much sleep for getting up to hand her a baby and changing wet or messy linens. He tried to wash the tiny boys gently when they needed it, and he took the smelly linens out of the room.

He didn't like the job, but he didn't hate it as much as he thought he would either. It made all the difference that these were his sons.

Twins. He had been doubly blessed. Now if Beth would just recover quickly.

He didn't even regret the distractions that caused him to get little sleep. He felt blessed to be taking care of his family. He did manage to nap some, and he doubted if he'd have slept at all if he hadn't been near Beth.

The next day, Stanton managed to get Beth to eat small amounts at each meal. Ida came over and helped all morning. When Mistress Ebert came to see Beth in the afternoon, Stanton went out to check on the farm. Ralph had taken care of everything, and nothing demanded his attention.

"She's improving fast," Mistress Ebert said. "To be honest, I wouldn't have given her much of a chance when I left yesterday. I'm glad to be wrong."

"I'm thankful, too."

"You keep her in that bed now, until the doctor gets here and says she can get up. With her nursing two babies, it'll be harder for her to get her strength back. I've given her all the instructions she should need, but, if you need me again, don't hesitate to send for me."

"Thank you, Mistress Ebert."

The following day, Stanton intended to work in the fields with Ralph until dinnertime, and then stay with Beth the rest of the day, but he couldn't do it. He couldn't leave her with Ida. He ended up going back to the house after less than an hour. She and the babies were like magnets. They pulled him back to them.

Not long after dinner, Mistress Denny came to call. She came up in her wagon, but she had a driver this time. The older man refused to come inside, and his mistress hurried toward the front door without introducing the man. She seemed to be a woman on a mission. She wanted to see Beth and the twins first thing. Stanton wondered if she'd make it up the stairs, but she did. He followed her into the room.

"Well, I declare. Aren't these the most beautiful little boys you've ever seen? Michael and Gabriel, isn't that right?"

"How did you know?" Beth asked.

Mistress Denny gave a huge grin. "Now there's not a whole lot going on around Middleville that I don't know about. For instance, I know your husband has stuck closer to you than ticks on a hound. I hear he's almost taken care of you all by himself. I like a man who's not too proud to see to his family like that."

"I think I have you to thank for pointing the sheriff in the right direction to find Horace Sneed," Stanton told her. He felt uncomfortable with her praise and wanted to shift the attention.

"Posh, just doing my duty as a citizen. By the way, Harold, who I left outside, is one of my brother's indentured servants. He's going to lend him to you for a few weeks to help Ralph so you won't have to worry about the farm. The man knows his farming, and he knows what to do and doesn't need directing."

Stanton gave her a warm smile. "How thoughtful of you, Mistress Denny. I'll be glad to pay your brother for Harold's time."

"Nonsense. This is my gift to your growing family, and it isn't costing me a thing. He came prepared to bed down in your barn, if that's okay with you. You tell Ida to expect him to take his meals with her."

"Yes, madam. I told her to cook for all of us over here at the house, until Beth gets on her feet. Harold will be welcome to join us."

Stanton noticed Beth's eyes twinkled, as if she fought to hold back her laughter. He almost laughed himself. Mistress Denny liked to take charge and command the day, but she had a generous heart.

"And, how are you doing, Beth? You're looking better than I expected after such an ordeal."

"I'm still too weak to do much, but I'm improving."

"Well, now, you do what Mistress Ebert and the doctor say. I want you to get well, now, you hear?"

"Thank you," Beth told the woman as she took her leave. "I'll recover faster with Stanton able to spend more time with me."

"Well, now, you be sure that you do, young lady. And you see that those two boys of yours get all the care they need too."

Harold turned out to be everything Mistress Denny said about him and more. He had a knack for organizing a farm and worked harder than someone half his age. Even Ralph seemed in awe of him, and Stanton hoped Ralph would learn something.

Beth recovered at a snail's pace, but she got a little better every day. When the doctor came exactly a week from when she'd had the twins, he pronounced she could begin sitting up an hour in the morning and an hour in the afternoon.

The twins were doing better too. Gabriel, who hadn't eaten well at first, had gained his appetite, and also seemed to be gaining weight. Michael, who couldn't get enough to eat, had settled down into a more regular routine.

It amazed Stanton how much of their character showed at only about a week and a half old. Michael would be the outgoing one who'd climb the trees to the top, swing the highest, and jump out of the barn loft. He'd be the curious, impetuous one. Gabriel would be quieter and more reflective. He'd be the one with a book in his hand, interested in figuring things out, observing more than taking part. Perhaps they'd be a good balance for each other and keep the other from getting too much out of kilter. He looked forward to seeing them develop.

After two weeks, the doctor gave Beth permission to be up as much as she wished, as long as she would rest if she became tired and take an afternoon nap, regardless. Stanton knew she didn't have as much stamina as she'd had before, but he thanked God every day for her progress.

He marveled at the love he felt. It remained a mystery to him how he could love Beth with his whole heart and still have room to feel the same for each of his children. And even more than all that, he had a growing love and trust for God. He could cry with David, "My cup runneth over."

He hadn't told Beth he loved her again because things had been so busy, and she'd been so weak and tired. He knew she'd ask him questions, and they needed a time to talk without distractions. With the two babies, such time became harder and harder to find.

Mistress Denny provided the answer. She had fast become one of their good friends. She came about a month after the twins were born.

"I figured you two could use a change and some time to yourselves," she announced. You send Ida over. She and I will take care of the twins and do some cooking and cleaning. Here"—she shoved a basket in Stanton's hands—"I've even packed you a dinner."

His heart jumped for joy. He had been looking for such a time when they both weren't so tired. So, they grabbed a blanket and walked hand in hand toward the forest. Stanton knew of a pretty meadow not far from the edge where they could have some shade but still face the glen.

"I'm tired of being idle," Beth said. "I'm going to start cooking and resuming my chores tomorrow. If I don't do some work soon, I'm afraid I'll never fully recover."

"Just promise me you won't overdo and have a relapse."

"I'll be careful." They walked quietly, and then she continued. "It seems strange to be away from the boys, doesn't it? They've become such a part of us."

"Strange but good. I've been wanting to have a serious conversation with you, but I've been looking for the right time."

"Have I done something wrong?"

The look of worry on her face wrung his heart. How could she believe he'd think she'd done anything wrong?

"No," he hurried to reassure her, "but perhaps I did. You almost died in childbirth, Beth. I don't want to take that chance again. I think we need to refrain from having more children."

"No, Stanton! Don't take that intimacy away. I need it; I need you. In fact, I'm ready to go back to the way things were before the twins were born. I want you to hold me and kiss me at night."

"We can still be intimate, darling. We'll just be more careful, and I'll need to take care of that. I'll show you what I mean soon."

"But I want to have more children. We're farmers. We need a big family, and I want a girl too."

"Beth, I don't think I could go through another delivery like that, and I'm not sure you could either."

"It won't be like that next time. The first is always the hardest, and I'm not apt to have twins again. Trust in God. He saw us through this time, didn't He? I'm fine, and we have two beautiful sons with only one birthing."

"I do trust in God more now. I had to in order to make it through that lengthy, complicated delivery. That's another good thing that came from all of this."

"Good. Then that's settled."

He couldn't help but laugh. "You're trying to influence and bend me to your will again, Beth Klein. I haven't agreed with you."

"No, I'm not. I'm just being logical, and you know deep down you agree with me. I know you would like to have other children too, and I also think you enjoy the trying." A mischievous glint sparkled in her eyes. "If you know how to keep me from getting in a family way again for a few months, that'll be good. But I refuse to give up having more children for long."

"I'll admit that you're right on those first two points. It's too hard for me to say no to you, especially to something I want too. But I would do anything for your well-being, Beth. I love you that much."

"Oh, my. That's what I thought you said to me after the twins came, but I wasn't sure. I thought I might have dreamed it."

"You didn't dream it. I said what came in my heart."

She reached over and took his hand, and he squeezed hers back. "When did you realize you loved me?"

"When I feared I might lose you. I've loved you for a long time, but I failed to realize it or admit it until then. You mean everything to me, Beth."

She kissed him tenderly on the cheek. "Just make sure I'm always second, and you put God first."

"For the first time in my life I can agree with that too, but I plan to spend the rest of my life showing you and telling you how much I love you. Come here. I hope you are at least strong enough for a real kiss."

Her eyes took on a delightful twinkle. "I'm not sure about that. Your kisses have a tendency of making me so weak I can't stand, even when I'm at my best."

He laughed, delighted with her teasing. "I'll carry you back to the house, if I need to."

At their study of the Bible that night, Stanton read the verses from 1 Corinthians 13, but he substituted the word *love* for *charity* because that's what Reverend Durk had said it meant.

"Though I speak with the tongues of men and of angels, and have not love, I am become as sounding brass, or a tinkling cymbal. And though I have the gift of prophecy, and understand all mysteries, and all knowledge; and though I have all faith, so that I could remove mountains, and have not love, I am nothing. And though I bestow all my goods to feed the poor, and though I give my body to be burned, and have not love, it profiteth me nothing. Love suffereth long, and is kind; love envieth not; love vaunteth not itself, is not puffed up, doth not behave itself unseemly, seeketh not her own, is not easily provoked, thinketh no evil; rejoiceth not in iniquity, but rejoiceth in the truth; beareth all things, believeth all things, hopeth all things, endureth all things. Love never faileth: but whether there be prophecies, they shall fail; whether there be tongues, they shall cease; whether there be knowledge, it shall vanish away. For we know in part, and we prophesy in part. But when that which is perfect is come, then that which is in part shall be done away. When I was a child, I spake as a child, I understood as a child, I thought as a child: but when I became a man, I put away childish things. For now we see through a glass, darkly; but then face to face: now I know in part; but then shall I know even as also I am known. And now abideth faith, hope, love, these three; but the greatest of these is love."

Stanton agreed, and these words took on new meaning. *The greatest is love.* He looked over at Beth and his two sons. It had taken him long enough to see it, but at least he finally had. Sometimes the love he felt for them almost overpowered him, but the love he felt for God proved even stronger. Somehow they all seemed connected. Maybe that's how it would always be when one lived in the center of God's will. Maybe this had been God's plan for him all along—to find love.

He'd say the prayer to end their time of devotion. Then he would take his wife to bed, where he could pull her into his arms once more.

"Great beauty, great strength, and great riches are really and truly of no great use; a right heart exceeds all."

—Poor Richard's Almanack

For more information about

Janice Cole Hopkins

Web page: **www.JaniceColeHopkins.com**

Email: **wandrnlady@aol.com**

Twitter: @J_C_Hopkins

Facebook: **www.facebook.com/JaniceColeHopkins**
(Please like this author's page)

If you enjoyed the book, please leave a review on Amazon or similar sites to let others know.

Made in the USA
Middletown, DE
30 September 2017